Great Love

Rida Allen

AmErica House
Baltimore

First printing

ISBN: 1-58851-024-7

PUBLISHED BY AMERICA HOUSE BOOK PUBLISHERS

www.publishamerica.com

Baltimore

Printed in the United States of America

<u>Dedicated To</u>
Roslyn and Frederick Neuman (Nana and Papa)
My parents Judy and Ted Milbach
My husband Robert
My brothers Michael, Alan and Bill
My aunt and uncle Fran and Sy Laskey
My best friend Heather Murray
And of course, to the dogs!
(Sugar, Crystal and Brandi)
Hey everyone, look, I'm a street sweeper!

Prologue

Parking her car, Samantha Velmar got out and tucked her keys into her purse. The small shopping center boasted several clothing stores, a few food establishments, a grocery store and an optician. The objective today was seemingly simple... purchase a couple of outfits for work. Granted, she could be relatively casual for her assistant manager's position at the bookstore, but preferred businesslike attire. And the small wardrobe she had needed to be rejuvenated with new additions.

She paused on the sidewalk, gazing at the mannequins in the store window. They sported fashionable pantsuits and skirts in bright, vivacious colors. While she stood in front of the display, a pair of younger women passed behind her. They looked from her, to the mannequin, and then at each other. As they walked away, they whispered furiously to each other and burst into laughter. With a sigh, Sam turned away and entered a store two doors down. The sign on the front announced boldly, 'Discount Fashions for the Larger Woman - Sizes 14+'.

Inside the store, there were racks and displays scattered about, leaving wide aisles for walking. Frowning, Sam passed several stands that had shirts with big floral prints and patterns. Toward the back, she found long, flowing dresses and thigh-length jackets that would compliment her 5'7" frame. She picked out several solid-colored dresses and a few jackets then headed for the dressing rooms located to the side of the shop. With a twist of the knob, she realized that the door was locked.

"Need some help, honey?"

Sam turned to find a petite brunette calling out to her from behind a rack of knit pants. "Yes, please. I'd like to try these on."

"Oh, sure." She approached and unlocked the door with keys attached to her wrist. "If you need any different sizes, you let me know. My name's Jamie."

"Thanks, Jamie." *Fat chance,* Sam thought to herself as she closed the dressing room door behind her. How could they have a plus-size store with a size 2 salesperson? There was no way she was going to tell her dress size to a woman who could fit her entire body into *one* of Sam's pant legs. Wasting no time, she tried on the different style dresses and decided on one. Once the dress was picked out, she reached for one of the black jackets and inspected the result.

"Doin' okay in there, hon?" a voice called out.

"Uh huh."

"How about tryin' on a pretty sun-dress with a matching button-sweater?" Jamie suggested. "They're all the rage now... good for a weekend at play or a barbeque."

"I don't think it would look right on me. Thanks, though."

"You'd be surprised! Let me just pick one out for your coloring... what size are you?" Jamie asked.

Cringing, Sam practically whispered her dress size through a crack in the door. She waited while the perky little Jamie went in search of said sun-dress.

"Here we go! This should do perfectly with your beautiful coloring." Jamie squeezed the outfit through the crack that Sam gave her in the door.

"Thank you." Shutting the door, she hung the dress on a peg and stared at it. What was that woman thinking? She would never have picked such a light beige color and with those pastel blue flowers! And the darker taupe-colored sweater was no match for her pale skin, she would look washed out with the whole combination! Rolling her eyes, she stripped off the dress she was going to buy and pulled on the tank-style sun-dress. It slipped over her head easily and was cool against her skin. Reaching for the sweater, she pulled it on as well and prepared for the worst.

"Ready to model for me?" Jamie's saccharin-sweet voice pealed out.

"Wha...?" the door to her dressing cube flew open and Jamie pulled her out into the open.

"Ooh! I knew it! With your beautiful auburn hair and that delicate skin, I just *knew* those colors would be great on you. And the length is just perfect... with some neat little strappy sandals, that's going to be a great outfit." Jamie cooed happily.

Sam turned back to the full length mirror and grudgingly had to agree. The color *was* perfect for her hair and skin. And with spring in full swing, she could even wear this to work. "Thank you for your help. For a moment, I thought you were crazy to bring this to me."

Jamie just grinned. "It helps to know what season you are, honey. You're a natural autumn, so your colors are really warm." Turning away from Sam, she clucked softly. "Such beautiful skin and such a pretty face..."

Sam frowned and returned to her dressing room to change back into her own clothes. Taking her selections with her, she approached the register. "I'm going to take this, too." she placed the dress and jacket on the counter, then reached for her wallet.

"Great!" Jamie began ringing up the clothes, as perky as ever. "You know, we have some great work-out clothes in the back, on sale!" she sang.

"Ah, no, this will be all."

As Jamie accepted Sam's credit card, another slender woman strode behind the counter. While she waited for approval, Jamie whispered something to the other salesperson.

Sam stiffened as the second woman glanced over at her, then looked away before replying to whatever Jamie had said. Heat filling her face, Sam signed her receipt, grabbed her credit card and practically bolted from the store. The last thing she heard as she was jogging out the door was a chipper, "Thank you! Come back soon!"

Once in the car, she stopped to catch her breath. The store had such good bargains and a good variety of clothes that Sam would have to ignore the salesperson's manners. But how awful it was to walk into a store meant for people her size and still feel uncomfortable! Maybe she would speak to the manager next time... Who was she kidding? She would never draw that kind of attention to herself.

Starting the car, she backed out of the parking spot and headed home, where she could be alone.

Chapter One

"This is ridiculous!" Jonathan slammed his fist against the wall and glared out the window. "How could my father be so... so... idiot!"

"Now Jonathan, you know your father loved you."

Jonathan glared at the paunchy lawyer sitting on the sofa. His balding head shimmered underneath the overhead lights as cigar smoke hovered around his face. "I'm beginning to think that he was crazy! And you, too, for going along with him, Simon!"

Simon harumphed around his cigar. "Your dad, he was in his right mind and that will is very legal and very binding."

"Barbaric is what it is! As if my whole life should revolve around creating a family." Jonathan grumbled.

"Your parents were very much in love for over forty years. I know for a fact that your father regrets waiting as long as he did to have you. He focused his whole life on his career and by the time you came along, he was not only older than he wanted, but he was also set in his ways when it came to work and his daily life." Simon explained.

"I never wanted for anything." Jonathan protested.

"Did you ever play ball in the back yard with him? Did he show you how to ride your first bike? Take you on your first camp out? Or go hiking or fishing or swimming in the lake?" Simon's voice was kind but his eyes were sad. "And here you are, twenty-nine going on sixty-five, with no life but this business. Your father married late, had you even later, and has now passed on before he could see you even begin to live. He wanted more for you."

Jonathan sank onto his chair. "Twenty nine isn't so old, Simon."

"But it will be before you know it." He stubbed out the remains of his cigar and pushed himself to his feet. "You have an entire year before the first stipulation of the will must be met. You're a handsome young man with a lot to offer. You'll be fine."

"What does my mother have to say about all of this nonsense?"

Simon reached for the doorknob, turning back to look Jonathan over. "You know your mother thought the sun rose and set on your father. She supported this like she supported everything else he ever said or did."

Jonathan nodded and rested his chin in his hand. "Yes, she did."

Simon opened the office door and stepped out, closing it softly behind him.

Jonathan barely noticed his departure. His parents' marriage had been full of love and devotion unlike any other he had ever seen or known. Even with the fourteen-year age difference, their marriage had been rock solid for forty-one years.

He never once considered marriage and here he was, being forced into it by a dead man in order to maintain control of the family business. A business that was his entire life. And worse yet, his mother held the final word on whether his 'relationship' was legitimate. While his mother may have been the 'good little wife', she was no pushover and knew all about true love. Damn that man!

Jonathan wiped the sweat out of his eyes as he rounded the corner of the indoor track. Running was as much a stress reliever for him as an exercise regimen. This indoor track and the modern health club in the basement of the office building was one of his ideas. It was free for employees, opened early and stayed open late into the evening to accommodate different schedules. Jonathan considered it one of the company perks that helped them maintain good people on the payroll.

One of the reasons he was running tonight was to try and work on a plan. He had no idea where to even begin looking for a wife. The thought of going to a bar to find a suitable woman was out of the question for him. What else did single people do? Should he scope out the vegetable aisle in the grocery store? Hang out in the lingerie section of the local department store?

What did he really want out of a life partner? Someone with intelligence, humor, passion and goals of her own. No offense to his mother, but he wanted a woman who had her own life, her own thoughts and her own mind.

But he needed to think farther ahead. Part two of the will indicated that he was to start his family within the first year of his marriage. So the woman he married would need to be loving, nurturing and most importantly, fertile.

Two days later, still stumped and concerned that time was slipping by, Jonathan went to visit his mother. On that particular Sunday afternoon, he found Alaria Edwards settled comfortably on the couch in the family room of her four bedroom colonial home. While large, the house was far from ostentatious. Alaria preferred the homey, lived-in look and her home reflected that in every room.

Alaria looked up from her book to find her one and only son standing in the archway. "Jonathan!"

A smile softened his face as he approached her and leaned over to kiss her smooth cheek. "Mom, how are you feeling?"

She touched his cheek. "Darling, I'm doing just fine. It's quiet, but I'm adjusting."

Jonathan settled onto the couch next to his mother. "I miss him, too."

"He adored you, Jonathan."

He gave her a wry smile. "He had a funny way of showing it."

She took his hand in hers. "You're so much like him. He was very aware of that. And while that pleased him to no end, it also worried him terribly."

"Didn't he have a good life, Mom?" he rubbed her fingers with his thumb.

Her voice softened. "He had a wonderful life and he would never have traded it for anything. But like any parent, he wanted you to learn from his mistakes. And with him being gone," her voice caught, "this was the only way he knew how to do that. He taught you very well when it came to business. But love and life, well, he just didn't know how to pass those lessons along to you."

"What if marriage isn't right for me, Mom?" he questioned.

She smiled. "You are your father's son, Jonathan. You have the heart for great love, you just need to realize it's there."

Frowning, he shook his head. "I have no idea how to find it."

"Don't go looking for it, sweetheart. Just open yourself up to the world, and it will develop before you know it." Alaria kissed her son's cheek and stood. "Please tell me you'll stay for dinner."

He stood with her. "You couldn't chase me away with lima beans." Smiling as she laughed at his least favorite food, he followed her into the kitchen.

Samantha opened the front door to her little house and sighed. Yet another customer had kept her late at the bookstore. She closed the door just as her eighteen month old golden retriever mutt came barreling around the corner.

"Molly!" Sam barely kept her balance as the rambunctious dog nearly knocked her over. "I'm so sorry, sweetie! I know I'm late."

Molly didn't seem to notice. Her every efforts were focused on tackling her mistress to the ground.

"Okay, okay! Just let me change and I promise you'll have a good long romp in the park." she sang as she stepped around the pooch and headed for her bedroom. "Go find your frisbee, Mol."

Molly's ears perked up at the mention of her favorite toy and she shot off into another room.

Jonathan eyed the green park from the safety of his car. Get out into the world, his mother said. Could he give up the security of his indoor track for this park? Would the trails be rocky and uneven, making his run dangerous? But then again, the weather was perfect, and dusk was his favorite part of the day. It was only one run, right? If he didn't like it, he could go right back to his track.

With the decision made, he opened the car door and got out. It took him a few minutes to figure out what to do with his carkeys, but once he tucked them away, he headed for a nearby bench to begin his stretching exercises. As he stretched, he looked over his surroundings. With some disappointment, he realized there were very few people in the park. Oh well, it was only one run, right?

Sam parked her car and turned to the dog panting excitedly beside her. "Okay, Mol, no knocking over any old ladies or little children."

Molly barked and licked her mistress' face.

Laughing, Sam opened her door and jumped out of the way as the big retriever tumbled from the little car. Fortunately, the park seemed pretty deserted at the moment. She grabbed Molly's frisbee and shut the car door with a thud. Walking toward an open, grassy area, she whistled once for her dog.

With great delight, Molly danced excitedly from one spot to another, waiting for Sam to throw the disc.

Jonathan was actually beginning to enjoy his run along the open fields. For a short span, the path wound its way through some trees. Moving at a good clip, he worked his way up a long hill. As he crested it, the setting sun came into view and he was almost mesmerized. He was so transfixed that he never saw the bright red object flying right at his head. He vaguely heard a shout before something struck him on the temple. The blow knocked him off-balance and he fell to the ground, cushioning the fall with his left hand.

"Damn!" he cursed, then ducked as a furry object jumped over him and retrieved the red object from the grass.

"Molly!"

Jonathan blinked and tried to focus on the direction the voice was coming from.

"Molly! Come here!"

Staggering to his feet, he turned just in time to be met with two big furry paws against his chest. With a shout, he landed on the ground again. He tried to cover his face to avoid being slobbered on, but to no avail.

Chapter Two

"Molly!" Sam's distressed voice finally got through to the mutt. She ran up the hill to find Molly sitting happily next to a very disheveled man. "Oh! Are you all right?"

"No thanks to you or your... your... beast here!"

Sam stopped short to stare at him. He was still sitting on the grass next to the path, his long muscular legs sticking out from his black running shorts. His dark brown hair was stuck to the crown of his head in sweaty clumps and his biting blue eyes were shooting daggers at her. "I'm so sorry!" she said, trying to contain her laughter at his description of Molly. "I warned her to stay away from old ladies and little children... I guess next time I should be more specific and mention joggers as well." *Especially extremely attractive joggers.*

He sniffed and got to his feet again. "Humph. Yes, well, you do that." he turned away, brushing dirt from the seat of his shorts.

Sam covertly appreciated the view for a moment, then said, "Are you sure you're okay?" She was absently patting Molly on the head, trying to keep her from running off again. "I saw the frisbee hit you pretty hard."

He rubbed his temple and shrugged. "I'll send you the doctor's bill."

A smile seemed to be tugging at the corner of his tense mouth. "Deal."

He studied her for a moment, and then remembered his manners. "My name is Jonathan."

She took his hand and shook it, reveling in his firm but gentle grip. "Samantha." Gesturing to her side, she said, "And this... beast, is Molly." Tugging on a lock of her long auburn hair, Samantha eyed his swelling left hand hanging limply at his side. "Jon, are you sure you're all right?"

He frowned at the shortened name and then gasped as she took his injured hand in hers. "What the...?"

"Oh dear, I hope it isn't broken!" she exclaimed, carefully cradling his hand.

His face softened at the concern in her voice. "I'm sure it's fine. No need to worry, Samantha."

"Sam." she corrected, still holding his hand.

With great care, he pulled his hand away and stepped back. "If the swelling doesn't go away, I promise to have it checked."

"Tomorrow." she pressed.

"Tomorrow."

Sam picked up Molly's frisbee and started for the parking lot.

Jonathan followed, trying to avoid stepping on Molly, who danced around and between them the entire time. He watched as Samantha, he couldn't conceive of calling her 'Sam', even in his mind, opened the door of an old two-door car. Without hesitating, Molly hopped in. Samantha leaned inside for a second, then returned to him at the sidewalk.

She took his good hand in hers and turned the palm upwards. Before he could protest, she began writing on the soft side of his arm. "Here's my phone number. Call me after you've seen your doctor so I know you're okay."

Jonathan stood mutely as she waved, got into her car and drove off. Looking down, he saw her first name and phone number printed neatly on his skin.

Before showering that evening, Jonathan transcribed her name and phone number into his phone book.

Stripping, he thought back to their encounter, replaying it in his mind. When she had come running up the hill, she had been slightly out of breath and sweat had gathered over her lip. Picturing her standing in front of him, he remembered her long auburn hair and warm chocolate colored eyes. She wouldn't be considered slender by today's standards, but seemed well proportioned and very soft.

Soft? What was he thinking?! With a grunt, he turned up the cold water before stepping into the shower.

Two days went by and Sam didn't hear from her mystery runner. As was her routine, she went to the park each night with Molly, but didn't see him again. Maybe he had been visiting from out of town and had gone home. Maybe he just wasn't interested in continuing any kind of conversation with her. After all, he hadn't even been out of breath from his run and yet her jog up the hill had left her panting and sweating.

Oh well, she was accustomed to being alone, doing things alone. It was just back to status quo for her.

For the third time that day, Jonathan's mind wandered from his computer screen to his telephone. His hand had recovered quickly and was back to normal size. Since he assumed that Samantha was only being courteous in giving her phone number, he hadn't bothered to call her.

Sighing, he turned back to the computer and squinted at the numbers there. He blinked and Samantha's face floated in front of his eyes. It was just plain rude of him not to phone her, right? After all, his parents had taught him proper manners... But wait, there were bigger obstacles to clear. Time was wasting away while he worried about some stranger's feelings. He needed to find a suitable and compatible woman. Someone warm, sweet, loving, soft, with thick auburn hair and all encompassing brown eyes...

Jonathan's hand thumped against the desk. What was he thinking? Where was his brain? She was perfect! Sweet and simple in her worn jeans and oversized tee shirt, warm and concerned over his well-being. And he already had the perfect opening. He reached for the phone and dialed the number already embedded in his brain. He hoped that she would forgive him for not calling right away. After ten rings with no answer, he hung up with a sigh. Maybe he could catch her in the park with a surprise?

Sam closed the front door and crossed the small foyer to her living room. She was just flopping down onto the couch as Molly came bounding around the corner.

"Hi Mol." Sam reached out to scratch the dog's head. "What a long day."

Molly whined and dug her nose into Sam's thigh.

"I don't think I can make it to the park, Molly." Sam sighed and closed her eyes. "Maybe we'll skip it tonight."

Molly barked and ran off, returning with frisbee in mouth.

"Oh, Mol, no." She sighed as Molly dropped the red disc in her lap. "All right, but you owe me!" Standing, she walked down the short hallway to her cozy bedroom. The entire house was one level, with only two bedrooms and two bathrooms, but was just ideal for her. The second bedroom was her den, since she never needed a guest bedroom. The house just met her needs and was just within her budget, so it was indeed perfect. Each square foot of the house was hers and no one else could lay any claim on it! She hadn't asked for anything from anyone since moving away from home at sixteen, and she never would!

With newfound energy, she turned to her dog. "C'mon, Mol, lets hit the park, baby!" Her comfortable jeans and tee shirt were both old and faded. "As a matter of fact, let's walk there!" Generally speaking she had no athletic leanings whatsoever, but how bad could the walk be? So she set out with Molly alternating between dancing at her feet and sniffing passing trees and bushes. By the time they reached the park, Sam knew she had made a mistake. She was exhausted and sweaty and dying of thirst. When they finally reached the grassy field, Sam dropped to the ground.

"I must be nuts!" With her last bit of energy, she tossed the frisbee in the air and let Molly go after it. Then she flopped backward into the fragrant grass and closed her eyes. How was she going to get home? Better yet, how was she going to get back up??!!

Jonathan's spirits sank when he didn't see Samantha's car in the parking lot. Maybe she was late or had car troubles. He got out of the car and closed the door, leaning against it's smooth exterior. As his eyes wandered over the park's hills and paths, a blur passed through his line of vision. Pushing away from the car, he headed for that spot, now hearing the insistent barking from just over the hill. As he came to the top, he spotted what he assumed was that beast, Molly, barking and nosing at something on the ground. Good Lord, that animal must have knocked someone else over and hurt them.

He looked around for Samantha as he trotted toward the dog. By the time he reached the scene, Molly had flopped down onto the ground. It took him a few seconds to realize what was in front of him. Fear gripped his insides as he dropped to his knees.

18

"Samantha!" She was so pale and still. His heart skipped a beat when one eye popped open to focus on him. "Are you all right?"

She laughed softly and opened both eyes. "Jon, how lovely to see you again. Excuse the mess."

He grabbed her wrist and felt for her pulse. "What happened?"

Pushing herself to a sitting position, she grinned tiredly at him. "I walked here before realizing how far away it was!" Smiling, she pushed her hair out of her face. "I just needed to catch my breath."

He sat back on his haunches and studied her. Her long auburn hair shimmered in the evening sun and framed her heart-shaped face. His eyes skimmed down over her generous chest, full shapely hips and long jean-encased legs. All of the sudden, he seemed to have some breathing trouble of his own.

"So, Jon, what are you doing here?"

He blinked and answered before he could consider the consequences. "Looking for you."

Her surprised gaze met his. "What?"

"Well," he got to his feet and held out a hand to help her up. "I wanted to repay you for your kindness and concern for me."

She eyed his hand for a moment before lithely rolling to her feet on her own. No way was she going to let him *haul* her to her feet. "It was my frisbee and my dog who tried to knock your block off," she grinned.

"That's simply irrelevant." Jonathan ignored her slight rebuff and started back toward the parking lot. "I've brought along a little surprise in the hopes that I would find you here."

"Well, you found me." she quipped.

He stopped under a big tree and turned to her. "Wait here." Without waiting for a response, he jogged to the parking lot and unlocked a low, sleek black car.

Sam watched with great interest as he pulled a folded blanket and a picnic basket from the back seat. Petting Molly absently, she tracked his movements back to her side.

"Would you hold this for a moment?" he handed her the heavy picnic basket before turning to spread the blanket over the soft ground. "Thanks." He took the basket back from her and set it in the middle of the blanket. "Shall we?"

She plopped ungracefully to the ground and instructed Molly to lay down on the grass next to the blanket.

Jonathan settled down next to Samantha and reached for the basket. "I hope you aren't a vegetarian."

Giving him a wry smile, she shook her head. "Nope."

"Great." he gave her a relieved smile. "I love a girl who can enjoy a juicy steak."

"You don't have a steak in there, do you?" she asked, her mouth already beginning to water.

He laughed. "Next time, I promise."

Her eyes widened as she wondered about 'next time'.

"Here we go." He unloaded containers of potato salad, cole slaw, pickles, two wrapped sandwiches that looked big enough to be hoagies, and a couple of cans of soda. Next he brought out plates and some silverware before closing the lid on the basket. He grinned at her, saying, "There might even be some dessert in there somewhere. Who knows?"

"This is very nice, Jon, but hardly necessary. A 'thank you' phone call would have been sufficient." she said softly.

He grimaced, then gave her an apologetic look. "I'm sorry about that. I tried to call you today, but there was no answer. Not even an answering machine picked up."

"That's good, because I don't own one."

"Well then, that would explain it. So, turkey or roast beef."

She pursed her lips in thought. "That's a tough choice."

He stared at her lips, wishing he had packed something stronger than cola.

"How about we split them?"

"Pardon?"

"We can each have half of one of the sandwiches. Compromise works every time." she grinned.

"Great idea."

"Ah, that was de-licious!" she crowed and flopped backward onto the blanket.

Jonathan smiled and eyed the half piece of chocolate layer cake on her plate. "Aren't you going to finish your cake?"

She groaned and slanted him a sideways look. "Be my guest."

Without hesitation, he grabbed her plate and quickly polished off the offending cake. "Yum."

Sam closed her eyes and stroked Molly's head. "Jon, you're a genius. This was wonderful."

Smiling, he looked over at her relaxed figure and froze. She was all curves, inviting hills and valleys that drew his eye and took his breath away. "Samantha..."

She didn't open her eyes. "Hmm?"

Before he could stop himself, he leaned toward her, inhaling her sweet smell. He stopped abruptly at the sound of a low, menacing growl.

Sam's eyes popped open. "Molly, what..." her voice trailed off at the sight of Jonathan mid-lean, his blue eyes smokey. "Jon?" she whispered, licking her lips.

Jonathan groaned. "I'm willing to risk the wrath of Molly if you are." he said hoarsely.

Her breath caught as he leaned closer. From her side, she heard Molly growl low in her throat again. As Jonathan lowered his head toward her, Sam gave Molly's muzzle a soft swat. The dog immediately fell silent.

Jonathan let out a soft puff of air before touching his lips to hers. He kept the kiss light but lingering, reveling in each second that passed. Her lips were soft and warm against his, making his heart pound at a furious rate.

Sam's eyes fluttered open as he pulled away. "Oh."

Jonathan felt a little out of breath. "Yeah, oh."

She pressed a hand to her runaway heart. "Jon..."

His eyes glittered at her flushed cheeks. "I'm still here, Samantha." Reaching out, he covered her hand with his. He felt her gasp at the touch of his hand.

Immediately she scrambled backward and sat up. "I have to go."

"Samantha, wait!" he held out a hand.

She froze but would not look at him.

"I'm sorry."

She shook her head mutely.

"I'm not sorry I kissed you." he laughed harshly. "Though my body may be later when I'm alone." His voice softened. "I'm sorry if I pushed too hard."

"I have to go." she repeated and stood. Molly followed suit, wagging her tail. "Thank you for the picnic. It was the nicest thing anyone has ever done for me." Grabbing Molly's frisbee, she turned away.

"Samantha," he jumped to his feet, "let me drive you home."

Her face was carefully blank when she turned back to him. "I can make it on my own, thank you." She turned and set off with Molly at a brisk walk.

Jonathan sighed and began cleaning up.

As soon as she rounded the corner, Sam let the tears fall. She could still feel his hand on her skin. It was too bad they had to stop because he really was a good kisser. She couldn't have asked for a more attentive, attractive and interesting companion. If only he weren't so perfect. She felt like a complete pig next to him. Even his jeans and polo shirt were pressed neatly and probably cost more than her weekly paycheck.

And even worse, every inch of his body was tanned, muscled, and finely toned. Her on the other hand... she looked down at herself and snorted. The walk from the park couldn't have been more than two miles of flat ground, and here she was, panting away, sweating at each step.

She would never be able to show herself in public with him. Everyone would snicker behind their backs, wondering what he was doing with the likes of *her*.

No, as usual, she was better off alone. "It's just you and me, Mol."

Molly wagged her tail in response and raced ahead to the house.

Chapter Three

All the next day, Jonathan kicked himself for crossing that invisible line with Samantha. He tried to phone her a few times, but each time his call went unanswered. He assumed that she was working, like any normal individual

He wanted to go to the park again to see her, but was afraid that he would frighten her away by showing up so soon. He needed to give her space, breathing room.

But what he really wanted to do was send her flowers. That he even had the thought, surprised him, but he didn't let it stop him. All he needed to do was find out her address. He already had her phone number, so that was a start.

With a frustrated sigh, Jonathan dropped the phone receiver back into its cradle. After fighting with the phone company representative and several supervisors, he got nowhere. It was 'against policy' to give out any address information based only on a phone number.

Jonathan frowned and buzzed his secretary.

"Yes, Mr. Edwards?" she spoke through the intercom.

"Miss Patrick, what florist do we use?" he asked.

"Welby's on Fourth." she answered. "Can I place an order for you?"

"No, thank you, I'd rather have the number."

She recited the seven digit number, then paused. "Are you sure I can't take care of this for you? It's no trouble."

"I think I can handle this." he told her in an amused voice.

"Sir, may I come in for a moment?"

Jonathan blinked at the speaker phone. "Of course."

The office door opened a moment later and his petite blond secretary entered. "Mr. Edwards," she said tentatively, "may I offer you a suggestion?"

"Shoot." he said pleasantly, leaning back in his chair.

"I'm guessing these flowers are for a... lady friend?"

Jonathan felt the heat stealing into his cheeks. "Well, yes, as a matter-of-fact, they are."

"Ladies are always touched by flowers..." she began, "but knowing your generosity..." her voice trailed off and she ducked her head at his intense stare.

"Go on..." he encouraged curiously.

"You may want to go with something a bit more simple than usual. Perhaps a colorful bouquet of wildflowers rather than the standard dozen red roses. Some ladies can be easily intimidated by a man who throws around a great deal of money..." she faltered.

He templed his fingers under his chin. "You may be right. She does seem like a wildflowers kind of lady." His eyes gleamed as he focused on her. "Thank you very kindly for your help. You're a smart lady, Miss Patrick."

She blushed and backpedaled out of the room, closing the door after her.

Jonathan picked up the phone and dialed Welby's. After identifying himself and asking for the manager, he began explaining his request.

"We have the perfect bouquet, Mr. Edwards. Very beautiful, very fragrant and very tasteful." the manager confirmed. "What is the address for your lady-friend?"

"This is where it gets difficult." Jonathan told him. "I only know that she goes to the Marcus Regional Park every evening around five thirty or six."

"Oh. Well, if you could give us an extremely detailed description of her, we could certainly *try* to deliver the flowers." he said hesitantly. "But I can't guarantee delivery."

"I understand. Charge me for the flowers either way." Jonathan confirmed. "Now, when you get to the park, she'll probably be in the field, playing frisbee with her dog. She has long reddish hair, brown eyes, a kind of round face. She usually wears faded jeans and a tee shirt. Her name is Samantha."

The manager repeated the description before asking, "What about a card, Mr. Edwards?"

Samantha danced around with Molly, teasing her with the frisbee. Molly barked and jumped around her, playing along happily. Sam released the frisbee just as she heard someone calling out. Turning, she spied a young man approaching with a beautiful bouquet of flowers.

"Excuse me, Miss." he called. "Are you Samantha?"

She raised an eyebrow at him questioningly and nodded.

"Well then, these are for you." he smiled and handed her the arrangement.

"What is this all about?"

"Beats me. But there's a card in there somewhere." he waved and jogged off.

Molly returned and dropped her frisbee, barking excitedly.

Sam looked around, expecting someone to jump out from behind a tree and shout, "Surprise, you're on candid camera!" When no one did, she turned the bouquet from side to side, looking for the card. She finally found it and pulled it carefully from the tiny envelope. She stopped briefly to throw Molly's frisbee again before unfolding the little card.

'Thank you for the wonderful evening yesterday. I hope I'll see you again soon... even if I have to let Molly knock me over again. (It would be worth it)'

The note was signed and a phone number was printed under the name. Sam looked around again, but saw no sign of Jon anywhere. Looking at the flowers again, she inhaled deeply, enjoying the fragrant bouquet.

It was a sweet gesture, but what did it really mean?

Jonathan slipped through the front door of his tidy apartment and dropped his keys on the hall table. He hurried to his answering machine and listened to the two messages there. Sighing in disappointment, he loosened his tie and picked up the phone to return his mother's call.

"Hello, Mom." he greeted her.

"Jonathan, darling, how are you?" she responded.

"I'm okay, thanks. How are you?" he sank gratefully into his leather easy chair, leaned his head back and closed his eyes.

"I'm fine, dear. The ladies are coming tonight for bridge. I fear my mind will not be on the game, but they are a forgiving brood." she laughed softly.

"It's good that they..." he was interrupted by a soft beep. "Mom, hold on a moment, would you? That's my call waiting."

"Of course."

Jonathan clicked over. "Hello?"

There was a pause. "Jon?"

His heart skipped a beat before settling back into its normal rhythm. "Samantha."

"Yes. How did you know?" she asked curiously.

"Would you hold on a moment?" he didn't wait for her reply but clicked back to his mother. "Mom, I'm sorry but I have another call..."

"Of course, darling. The ladies will be here soon anyway."

"Have a good game, Mom." he said absently.

"Love you." she blew him a kiss and hung up.

His hand shaking slightly, he clicked back over to Samantha. "Hello?"

"Hi."

"It's good to hear from you." He closed his eyes and let her voice envelop him. "How are you?"

"I'm good, thanks." she paused. "Thank you for the flowers. They're quite beautiful."

So are you, he thought to himself. "You're welcome. Thank you for having dinner with me. I had a very good time."

"So did I. You're a very conscientious person to go this far to thank me."

Frowning, he considered his answer before speaking. "Samantha, I sent you the flowers because I wanted you to have them. It has nothing to do with getting hit by your frisbee."

She was silent for a moment. "I see."

"Do you?" he asked, getting up to pace the length of his living room. "Do you see that I enjoy your company and want to get to know you better?"

She chewed on her lip and stared at the flowers on her dining room table. How was she supposed to answer that?

"Samantha?"

She opened her mouth but no sound came out.

"I don't want to press you." he said softly. "But I would like to see you again."

"Jon..."

He chuckled softly to himself, realizing that he was beginning to enjoy her use of that name. It felt warm and intimate. "You don't have to answer now. We can just talk."

"All right, we can talk, if that's what you want." she answered.

"I'll take what you're willing to give, Samantha." *For now.* "If friendship is what you're offering, then I'm taking." He smiled and sank back into his chair. "So how is Molly tonight?"

Jonathan whistled happily as he entered his reception area. "Good morning, Miss Patrick." He gave her a big smile and handed her a bright yellow rose. "Thank you for your advice."

"It worked out well, then?" she sniffed the rose appreciatively.

"Very well, very well." he said before going into his office. Last night turned out as well as he could have expected at this point. They had talked for about ninety minutes, and he had enjoyed every second of it. He learned more about her, including about her job at the book store. In turn, he told her a little about his work and his interests, which happened to include a large library of books. They quoted famous books back and forth for a while before moving on to a new topic. Jonathan found out that she was not only a dog lover, but was adamant about supporting the humane society, which is where she found Molly at four months old.

She was sharp as a tack with a humorous wit that amused and delighted him. If only he could get past whatever her reservations were about him and/or a relationship with him. He was going to have to show her, to prove to her that he was a good man. He was going to do everything he could to show her that he was the right man for her. He needed to show her that what was important to her, was important to him. With a smile, he picked up the phone.

Sam smiled as she walked through her front door. It was almost two weeks since she first met Jonathan in the park and since that wonderful first phone call, they spoke every evening. She was getting accustomed to her new evening routine and was generally curled up with a book when he called. She was hoping that tonight wouldn't be any different.

Jon was turning out to be a wonderful friend, thoughtful, intelligent, and caring. He never failed to ask her about her day and the events at the bookstore.

Sighing, she admitted to herself that she was looking forward to hearing his deep, warm voice. Something about it made her feel cherished and desired. Jon listened to her with an intensity that blew her away, even when she blathered on about Molly.

Sam dropped her mail on the coffee table and whistled for Molly. "C'mon Mol, let's hit the park! I only have a couple of hours before Jon calls."

Sam and Molly returned from the park, tired but happy. Since the picnic, they had started walking to and from the park. While Sam doubted that the walk was making any difference in her physical appearance, it was certainly getting easier every evening.

Not wanting to waste any more time, she raced for the shower to ready herself for the evening. She didn't want to explore her excitement over a silly phone call... she just wanted to enjoy it.

After her shower, she sat down to have a quick dinner. She never really minded cooking and was fairly adept at it, but cooking for one just wasn't worth it. Maybe someday she would have someone to cook for.

Molly munched happily on her dog food in the corner of the kitchen, paying no attention to her mistress' humming at the kitchen table.

Knowing that Jon would be calling within the hour, Sam padded into the living room and curled up on the sofa. The unopened mail sat within arm's reach on the coffee table, but she just didn't have the energy to deal with it right now. That hot shower was making her sleepy so she decided to close her eyes for just a few minutes.

Jonathan settled onto his easy chair and picked up his cordless phone. He looked forward to his nightly calls with Samantha, but now he was starting to want more. He had already decided that tonight was the night he was going to ask her out on their first official date.

Dialing her number, he leaned his head back and closed his eyes. After six rings, he started getting nervous. Did he do something wrong? Was she avoiding him? She finally picked up on the tenth ring.

"H... hello?"

Jonathan's relaxed body responded immediately to her sleepy, sexy voice. He exhaled slowly before speaking. "Samantha?"

"Mmm, Jon? What time is it?"

He shuddered, wishing he could crawl inside her voice. Better yet, wishing he could crawl inside her and stay there forever. Groaning, he shifted in his chair. "It's nine-fifteen, honey."

She yawned loudly. "I guess I fell asleep. I didn't mean to. I was looking forward to hearing from you."

"Me, too." he responded softly. "So how was your day honey?"

"It was lovely."

Jonathan smiled, hearing the soft sleepiness in her semi-conscious voice. "Did you and Molly get to the park this evening?"

"Yeah."

If only he could be beside her to enjoy this sleepy evening. She sounded so comfortable, so content. He was just dying to hold her in his arms, breathe in the clean, freshly showered scent of her. To press kisses to her temple and her lips, to smooth the soft hair away from her face.

"Jon?"

Her sweet voice pulled him from his private thoughts. "I'm still here, sweetheart."

"I love the sound of your voice. I hear it in my dreams, you know." she murmured.

His eyebrows shot up. Did she think this was all part of a dream? "Are they good dreams, Samantha?"

"Mmm, yeah."

He swallowed hard and wondered if he would ever recover from this conversation. "Do I touch you in your dreams, sweetheart?" his voice was low and husky.

"Yeah." she sighed. "You have such strong and gentle hands."

His free hand curled into a fist and he thumped it against his thigh. She was totally out of it and he was more turned on than he had ever been in his entire life. "Oh, baby, I love touching you."

"And your lips are so soft against mine." she whispered.

Jonathan nearly sobbed out loud. "Samantha, honey, you need to wake up before I pass out from the lack of blood in my brain."

"Mmm."

"Okay, sweetie, why don't you put the phone back down, snuggle up and go back to sleep." he told her.

"Mmm."

"Go on, Samantha, hang up the phone."

"Jon..."

"Good night, baby." He released a deep breath when he heard the soft click of the phone in his ear. Dropping the phone with a clatter, he headed for a nice, long, cold shower.

Chapter Four

Sam tried to roll over and nearly fell off the couch. "Oh!" She woke with a start, struggling to grasp her whereabouts. Sitting up, she saw the unopened mail still on the table, the phone next to it and Molly asleep on the floor.

"Oh, no! What time is it?" She shot to her feet and raced into the kitchen. The clock on the microwave said eleven twenty-five! What happened? Did he call?

She gathered up her mail and took it with her into her bedroom. Could she call him at this hour of the night? She missed him, even dreamt about him.

Absently she began sifting through her mail and found something from the local humane society. As she was ripping it open, Molly wandered into the room, jumped up on the bed and curled up to sleep again. Sam patted her soft head and pulled the card from its envelope. The hand written note shocked her.

'Dear Miss Samantha Velmar,
This is to inform you of a substantial donation made to the humane
society in the name of your dog, Molly. We thank you and the
contributor, Mr. Jon Edwards, for your support and generosity.
Without people like you, we would not be able to continue our much
needed work. We thank you sincerely.'

Sam covered her mouth with her hand. Without thinking of the late hour, she picked up the phone and dialed Jon's number. He answered after only one ring.

"'Lo?"

"Jon." she breathed. She heard his startled intake of breath.

"Samantha, what are you doing awake at this hour?" he asked.

"I was just going through my mail."

"Oh?"

"Don't sound so innocent, mister." she scolded him. "You are an incredibly sweet man."

He smiled. "Why thank you, ma'am."

"I'm so touched that you did this."

"I wanted to do it. You make a very good case for what those people do." he explained.

"I'm sorry I missed your call earlier. I hope you weren't worried about me."

"No," he said softly. "I wasn't too worried about you."

"I must have fallen asleep. I only remember wanting to close my eyes for a few minutes." she laughed.

"You were tired. I hope you feel better now." his voice was low and smooth.

"I do, now that I'm talking to you." she told him.

"Samantha, I want to see you again." he said suddenly.

"What?" panic laced her voice.

"I don't want to press you, but I would like to see you. I feel like it's been forever since I've seen your face." He paused. "Let me cook you dinner. I make a mean steak."

She pondered his request. "Steak, huh?"

"And a big baked potato."

"Well..."

"Saturday night. I'll come get you at five thirty." he suggested.

"You can give me directions and I'll drive myself." she countered.

"That is a deal."

"Molly! What have I done? I can't go over there, be alone with him!" Sam wailed.

Molly wagged her tail from her comfortable position on Sam's bed.

"Some help you are!" She stuck her tongue out at the dog and dove back into her closet. Pants, a skirt, heels, hose, a dress, what? After pawing through everything in her closet, she settled on a long, dark purple skirt and matching thigh-length top. She knew the plum-like color was good for her hair color and skin tone. She slid on panty hose and short-heeled pumps.

"Well, it's going to have to do." Patting Molly on the head, she picked up her purse and keys and headed for the door.

The drive to Jon's apartment seemed to take forever, but finding a space in the parking lot was easy because the lot was relatively empty. The lobby of the high-rise building was very well appointed, giving her a hint of what was to come. While the elevator whisked her quickly up to the eleventh floor, she had plenty of time to have second thoughts. When the muted 'ding' announced her stop, she emerged cautiously, looking first down one direction of the hallway, then the other. It took her a few minutes to find the door marked 1114, and a few more moments to work up the courage to knock.

Almost immediately, the door swung open and Jonathan was filling the doorway.

"Hi." he greeted her with a wide smile, grabbed her hand and drew her into the apartment.

"Hi, Jon." She couldn't tear her eyes off his incredible face.

Touching her cheek with his free hand, he caressed her soft skin. "You look beautiful."

Sam could feel the blush spreading over her face. "You look pretty darn good yourself." He was wearing dark gray slacks and a white oxford shirt, unbuttoned at the throat and rolled up his muscular arms to his elbows.

His hand smoothed along her skin and cupped her cheek. "I'm so glad to see you."

She shifted her weight and took her first look around the apartment. "Wow, this is nice."

Stepping back, he let his right hand drop but kept his left clasped with hers. "Thanks. Want the nickel tour?"

"Sure." The apartment was large and airy and very well decorated. There was a powder room off the foyer, the master bedroom and bathroom, a spacious living room with a gas fireplace, a separate dining room and a nice-sized kitchen.

Stopping in the kitchen, she inhaled sharply. "The potatoes smell good."

He smiled. "Not to worry, I haven't tried to trick you. I'll put the steaks in shortly. Would you like a drink?"

"Just some ice water, please." she responded, wandering back into the living room. Dropping her purse on the floor next to an end table, she crossed the room to the fireplace.

"Here we are." He strode to her side and handed her the tall blue glass. "I put the steaks on. They won't take long."

"Thanks." she took a sip of the water and surveyed the room. "You certainly have nice taste in furniture." The big leather couch probably cost more than her monthly mortgage.

"I like to be comfortable." was his only reply. "Would you like some music?"

"Sure." She moved to perch on the edge of the couch as he crossed to the stereo on his entertainment center. Glancing around surreptitiously for a coaster, she spotted them stacked on the end table. She separated one from the pack, then set her glass down.

Jonathan turned to face her as soft jazz filled the room. "I hope this is all right."

She smiled and looked away as he came to join her on the couch.

"Samantha," he took her hand in his. "Are you as nervous as I am?"

Her surprised eyes shot up to meet his wry smile. "Yes."

"Well, we should stop that right now. After all, your dog has drooled all over my face!" he grinned.

"And I'm sure you enjoyed every minute of it." she snickered at the face he made.

Suddenly, he stood and held out his hand. "Will you dance with me?"

"What?"

"Dance. Nothing fancy, mind you." he teased. "Otherwise you might not walk away with all of your toes."

"I don't know..."

"C'mon, it'll be fun." he held her hand as she got to her feet and followed him out in front of the coffee table. He drew her into his arms, letting her set the distance between them.

Soulful jazz wound its way around the room, seeming to fill every corner. As Samantha relaxed in his arms, he began to draw her closer. He worked slowly, knowing he would stop at the least sign of resistance.

The song came to an end and Jonathan released her reluctantly. "I should check on the steaks. I'll be right back." He touched her cheek gently before heading for the kitchen.

Sam exhaled slowly and whirled away to inspect the books on his shelves. If she were smart, she would plant herself right on that couch and refused to budge until dinner. But truth be told, she really enjoyed being in his arms. He made her feel like she was floating on air.

"A few more minutes and we'll be ready to eat." he told her.

"All right."

He stepped into the middle of the room and held out his hand. "Where were we?"

A tentative smile formed on her lips as she took his hand and practically glided back into his arms. He was a good five inches taller than her, making his shoulder look like an inviting resting place. As they danced, she felt herself drifting closer, as if she were being drawn into his embrace.

Jonathan heaved a contented sigh as her lush body brushed, and then melted into him. He curled their clasped hands against his chest as her head came to rest on his shoulder.

The music swirled around them, enveloping them in a cloak of sound and beat.

Jonathan turned his head and pressed a light kiss to her temple. Her feet faltered once before regaining their smooth rocking motion.

All of the sudden, everything seemed to happen at once. The cd clicked off, the oven timer buzzed and the phone rang.

He stepped away, his hand lingering in hers before releasing her. "Would you mind grabbing the phone?" He left to get the steaks.

Sam grabbed the cordless phone off the table next to the recliner. "Hello? Oh, um, Edwards' residence." she sputtered.

"I'm looking for Jonathan. May I speak with him?" The woman's voice was pleasant and unperturbed at a female answering the phone.

"May I tell him who is calling?" Sam asked politely.

"Alaria."

"I'll see if he's available." Hugging the phone to her chest, she trotted into the kitchen. "It's Alaria."

Jonathan looked up from the stove. "Oh. Thanks." He took the phone from her and balanced it between his ear and shoulder. "Hi, Mom."

Sam released the breath she was holding. *Mom.* She left the kitchen, giving him some privacy.

Jonathan grinned into the phone. "Mother, don't get all excited. I've gone on dates before, you know."

"Now, darling, I never had any doubt that you would find a wonderful woman to help you fill your life." she whispered loudly.

"Mom, you're on the other end of the phone, you don't need to whisper."

Her tinkling laugh floated over the line. "Is she wonderful? How long have you known her? When do I get to meet her? Is her family in the area? How old is she? Has she been married before? She doesn't have children already, does she? What does she do for a living?"

"Mom, please! I *am* right in the middle of the date, you know. If I don't hop to it, she may leave without tasting my fabulous steak! And it will all be for naught. Do you want that hanging over your head?" he teased her.

"No, no, no. You go right ahead and enjoy your dinner. Do call me later." She said, in a falsely mild voice.

"Love you Mom." He pressed the off button and dropped the phone in its charger. He carried the baked potatoes and vegetables into the dining room, then returned with the steaks. "Samantha." he called to her from the dining room. "We're ready to eat."

She stepped into the room, sniffing appreciatively. "Smells yummy."

Jonathan held out her chair for her and waited for her to get comfortable before seating himself. "Would you like any wine?" he offered.

"No, thank you."

"Well, dig in."

Rubbing her hands together, Sam reached for her silverware. "So, how is your mother? I hope she's not too lonely." Jon had told her a few nights ago about his father's recent passing.

"No, I think Mom's friends have really rallied around her." He cut into his steak. "She's an active and fun lady and I'm sure she'll get back into the swing of things soon."

"Do you think she'll ever remarry? She's still quite young, isn't she?"

Her question was innocent enough, but it still made Jonathan stop in his tracks. "I guess I never thought about it. Mom and Dad were so desperately in love that I can't imagine her with anyone else. But," he said softly, "if she ever finds someone who makes her happy, I sure hope she'd go for it. She would never expect any less of me."

Sam looked up at him, the candles on the table flickering across her face. "What a wonderful thing to say. I hope someday in the future you'll be able to tell her that. I'm sure she would be touched and proud."

"Mom is a wonderful lady and I want nothing but the best for her." He smiled at her. "What about your family? I know they aren't in the area, but are you close?"

Her expression closed almost abruptly. "No, we aren't."

Jonathan blinked, then wished he had kept his mouth shut. Her lips were drawn tightly and her shoulders stiffened. "I'm sorry." He wanted nothing more than to wipe the pain away for her, but knew somehow that the wound was deep and long.

She gave him a wan smile and dove into her baked potato with false cheerfulness. "You sure know how to bake 'em, buddy."

To Samantha's utter dismay and Jonathan's delight, she cleaned her plate without any further hesitation. Fortunately, he did the same, and then some by helping himself to seconds with the crunchy, tasty vegetables.

"You do cook a mean steak, sir." she informed him, leaning back in her chair. "That was the best steak dinner I've eaten in a long time."

"Really? You don't cook steak for yourself?" he asked, balling up his napkin and tossing it onto the table.

"I can't really afford such luxuries." she said softly, staring at her empty plate.

"Well, that makes this one all the more special." he got to his feet and began clearing away the dishes.

Sam raised her eyebrows, but stood and helped him carry dishes into the kitchen.

"I'll take care of these later." he waved at the mess before taking her hand and leading her back into the living room. "Let's get comfy. It's nearing our phone call time." he teased.

Smiling, she kicked off her shoes and curled up into his side on the couch. "This is much nicer than my lonely old sofa."

He sighed and settled his arm around her shoulders. "So, how was your day?"

Sam giggled. "You're not going to ask me about the bookstore, are you?"

He turned his head to gaze into her dark, expressive brown eyes. "No, I do believe I'm going to ask you if I may kiss you."

"Oh."

He touched her chin, tilting her head up. "May I?"

Her gaze dropped to his lips. "Oh, yes."

He released the breath he was holding and leaned forward to press his lips to hers. He could feel her hand tentatively touching his stubble-roughened cheek as his lips moved gently over hers. When he pulled away, he heard her murmur his name.

"Jon..." ·

He got to his feet, leaving her almost abruptly, as his body responded to her, her lips and her breathy voice.

She looked up at him sadly, but not accusingly. After all, why would he want her? She was still roly-poly Sam, destined to be dumpy forever. "It's okay. I'll go now."

Kneeling down in front of her, he took her hands in his. "You're the only person in my entire life who ever called me Jon. I've always been Jonathan to everyone who ever knew me. Hearing you call me Jon," his voice grew husky, "just reminds me how much this part of me belongs to you."

She looked at him almost fearfully. "What do you mean?"

"Samantha, my heart belongs to you, my soul belongs to you. This part of me that is able to experience love, belongs only to you. You brought it out of me. I never even knew it was there before I met you." he whispered, holding her hands tightly, fearing she would run away.

"Jon..."

He groaned and pressed a kiss to her clenched hands. Joining her on the couch again, he pressed her head forward into his chest. He gently kneaded the back of her neck under her thick curtain of hair. "Samantha, before you say anything, let me just finish what I want to say." He paused. "I'm not asking for anything from you... for now. I just want to continue spending time with you, as we are now. Whatever time you are willing to spend with me, I'll cherish. No strings, no pressure." He drew her head back to rest against the couch so he could see her face. "Are you comfortable with what I'm asking of you?"

She looked up into his clear blue eyes, wondering just when she had become his completely. "Yes." she whispered.

A smile spread over his entire face, lighting up his eyes. "May I kiss you again?"

Her answer was to pull his head down to meet her waiting lips.

Chapter Five

Monday morning, Sam pushed her head out from under the covers at seven a.m. and reached for her bedside phone. She dialed Jon's number at work. After the fifth ring, someone picked up.

"Edwards here."

His voice was annoyed. "Tsk, that's not a very professional way to answer your phone."

"Samantha?"

She smiled sleepily and snuggled deeper into her bed. "Good morning."

"Good morning, sweetheart. What are you doing up so early?" he asked.

"Who says I'm up?"

He groaned. "You're still in bed."

"Yup."

"That's just mean," he growled at her. "How will you ever make it up to me?"

"By taking you to lunch today."

"I think that will do. Meet me here at 12:30." he instructed.

"Okay. Are you sure you can get away today?" she asked him.

"I'll make sure I can get away." he groaned again. "I'd better go, honey, before my secretary finds me in this uncomfortable state at her desk."

She stiffened at this comment. "What?"

He chuckled and lowered his voice. "I'll see you later. Bye, Samantha." he disconnected without waiting for her response.

Frowning, she hung up the phone and reached out to pet Molly's soft back. "Why would he say that, Mol?".

Since it was her day off from the bookstore, Sam puttered around the house for a while. But each time she got involved in something, Jon's words drifted back to her. Maybe he was just trying to make her feel desired. Intellectually she could understand him being attracted to her as a person. And lord knew that he turned her on, but for him to have that kind of response to her? She would never believe it.

With a sigh, she finished scrubbing the kitchen sink and went to clean up for lunch.

The drive to Jon's downtown office took just over half an hour, but Sam still arrived early. She parked her car in a visitor's space and slid from the vehicle. Last night he had told her that the offices were on the third floor and the main receptionist could direct her to his secretary.

The woman at reception was cheerful and pleasant when she directed Sam to Jon's offices at the end of the long hall. "Miss Patrick will buzz Mr. Edwards for you."

"Thank you." Sam walked briskly along the hallway, aware of eyes following her from offices on either side. She had only thrown on dark blue slacks and a pale pink blouse for their lunch, now she wished she had done more. As she neared Jon's office, her heart sank. The petite, pretty blond behind the desk looked up at her approach.

"May I help you?" she asked formally.

"Is Mr. Edwards in?" Sam's voice was timid.

"He's in a meeting. Do you have an appointment?"

Sam opened her mouth to answer, her hands clutched together in front of her when Jon's door flew open.

He walked out with another man, his face intent and serious. They shook hands and the man turned and left. Jon was just turning to his secretary when he spotted Samantha. His entire face lit up and he crossed to greet her.

"Samantha!" He grasped her by the shoulders and pressed a quick kiss to her lips. "You look beautiful."

She blushed and let her hand rest on his arm.

"Mr. Edwards?"

Jonathan turned back to his secretary. "Miss Patrick, this is Samantha Velmar. Samantha, this is my indispensable secretary, Miss Patrick."

Sam murmured her hello.

The secretary frowned. "Did I forget to schedule an appointment, sir?"

"No, of course not!" he laughed and slid his arm around Samantha's waist. "Samantha is here to take me to lunch." He winked at her before turning back to his secretary. "We'll be back in a little while."

"But your afternoon appointments!" she called after them.

"I won't be late, don't worry." he called back, guiding Samantha past the front reception area and out the front door.

"Your secretary seemed a little upset." Sam said, hurrying to keep up with him.

"She's very conscientious about her work. I guess I forgot to tell her about our lunch." he replied, walking with her toward a nearby deli.

She frowned, remembering the pixie-like woman staring at her when she had first approached the desk. "Oh."

"This is so nice." he said as they sat down with their trays.

She smiled wanly.

"I've been having trouble concentrating all morning, thinking about you." he grasped her hand on the table. "I just want to play hooky all day and spend it with you."

Relaxing a little, she laughed softly. "Is that how your dad built his great business? By playing hooky?"

He gazed at her intently. "Nope. But the business is definitely at a different point in its life then when my dad was my age. I can afford to take a couple of days off here and there."

"Must be nice, buddy." she teased.

He grinned and reached for his sandwich. "Yup."

Jonathan walked Samantha to her car. "Thank you very much for lunch. I had a fabulous time." Stopping at her car, he pulled her into a hard hug.

She hugged him back, enjoying the feel of his strong arms around her. "We should do it more often."

"Yes, we should." He pressed a quick kiss to her soft lips. "Drive carefully going home."

"I'll talk to you tonight?" she asked.

"I wouldn't miss it for the world." he helped her into her car, then watched her drive away. He could still smell her perfume clinging to his skin and clothes. As he walked back to his office, he wondered what it would be like to go home to Samantha every evening. To have her soft arms and sweet scent envelop him every night. Checking his watch, he groaned and strode quickly back to his office.

"Mr. Edwards..." his secretary began.

He flashed her a smile. "I'm late, I know. Did you get him some coffee?"

She nodded and handed him a folder on his way past.

Wednesday afternoon, Jonathan called Samantha at the bookstore. "Hi honey." he greeted her.

"Jon, what a nice surprise!"

"What are you doing this evening?"

"Nothing special. Why, do you have something in mind?" she asked.

"I'll pick you up after work. Five-ish?"

"Okay." She hung up after saying goodbye. Now why hadn't he told her where they were going? She hadn't seen him since lunch on Monday so she was looking forward to five o'clock. Suddenly she was glad she wore one of her nicer outfits to work today.

The next two hours flew by quickly while Samantha restocked the paperback section. Before she knew it, Jon was walking through the front door. Smiling, she waved and headed for the back room to get her purse. She stopped and bid goodnight to one of the store's owners before joining Jon up front.

"So," he whispered, "which one is here?"

Samantha giggled and pushed him out of the shop. "Is that why you came down here?"

Laughing, he threw his arm around her shoulders. "You have to admit, twins born four minutes apart, on May 31st and June 1st named May and June are definitely a sight to see!"

She poked him in the side as they neared his car. "So, what are we going to do?"

"Let's get in the car." he handed her into the car and rounded the front to get in on the driver's side.

"What's going on?" she turned in her seat to face him.

"I want to buy you a dress." he blurted out.

Her eyebrows shot up. "What?"

"Let me rephrase that." Smiling, he ran his hand along her hair. "There's a black-tie dinner Friday evening that I need to attend and I want you to go with me. I thought you might like to have a new dress."

She pursed her lips and considered his offer. "Jon, I'm not sure I'm comfortable with you buying me a dress."

"Just this once." he promised.

"Look, Jon, maybe you should take someone else. I'm sure your secretary would have appropriate attire." she sat back in the seat and crossed her arms over her chest.

"Miss Patrick?" he was flabbergasted. "Honey, if you won't go with me, I'll have to go alone. I have absolutely no interest in my secretary or anyone else besides you."

Her face softened at the hurt in his voice. "I just don't want to embarrass you in front of your colleagues."

"With you by my side, I expect to be the envy of all the male attendees." he told her, stroking her cheek gently. "It would be a great honor for me if you would accompany me Friday night."

She covered his hand with hers. "All right."

"Great!" he grinned, kissing her hand. "My mom loves this boutique on Montrose Avenue. Let's go there first."

Sam's shoulder stiffened. "Jon..." she began as he started the car.

"It's a great place and Madame Vue said she had plenty of time to see us this evening." he said cheerfully.

She groaned and turned to stare out the window. This was sure to be a disaster.

A few minutes later, they pulled up in front of the fashionable storefront.

"Here we are!" He shut off the car and turned to smile at her. When he saw her pained expression, he turned her face toward him. "Samantha, trust me to take care of you, all right?"

She gave him a brave smile and slid from the car. By the look of the mannequins in the windows, she was sure 'Madame Vue' was going to take one look at her and laugh her skinny little butt off.

Jonathan pulled her through the front door and called out, "Madame, where are you?"

"Oui, I am coming!" a heavily accented voice called back. A moment later, a woman burst into the room and engulfed Jonathan in a hug. "Oh, you sweet boy!"

He grinned over her head at Samantha. "Bonjour, Madame."

She pinched his cheeks before turning to face Samantha.

Sam couldn't help but smile at the woman. Contrary to her worries, Madame Vue was a short, round woman with neatly coifed hair and a contagious smile. "Hello."

"Madame Vue, this is my... er, Samantha Velmar." Jonathan introduced them.

The older woman grabbed his arm and squeezed hard enough to make him grimace. "Jonathan, she is beautiful!" she swatted his shoulder. "You did not do her justice, non!"

Sam's eyes flew to his amused face.

"Oui, you come with me, belle. I have perfect dress for you. Jonathan, sit!" she instructed before pushing Sam through a curtain to an opulent fitting room. "It is perfect for you. Sweetheart neckline to enhance your bosom." she indicated her own generous chest before scurrying off into a back room.

Studying the room, she saw several full-length mirrors, a few curtained changing rooms and an ornate couch against one wall, where she dropped her purse.

"Here, here!" Madame burst back into the room with a black gown in her arms.

"The size..." Sam began, stepping forward.

Madame scoffed at her. "Samantha, cherie, I am professional at this business! You go behind curtain and put this on. Come out and I zip for you." She pushed the dress into Sam's arms and shooed her into a changing room. "I be back with perfect shoes."

Sam grimaced as she slipped out of her clothes. There was no way this woman was going to just *have* an evening gown that would fit her. Carefully she hung up her clothes and pulled the black gown on over her head. It seemed to be a simple, matte black dress that fell to just below her ankles. She was surprised to see a high slit up along her left leg. Peeking around the curtain, she saw Madame standing across the room, so she stepped out.

"Madame, I can't..."

"Oui, oui, I zip for you." she pulled Sam into the middle of the room.

"This top, I can't wear this." Sam indicated the sleeveless bodice.

"Oh, the line is beautiful. Here is the jacket." Madame helped her into the tailored hip-length tuxedo-style jacket. The lapels and the trim of the jacket were a shiny satin material. She slid her hands along Sam's side and over her hips to show her the sleek line. "See the beautiful silhouette shape. You have perfect shape for this! I just knew it! Put on these heels and let us look."

Sam was almost mesmerized by the woman who was staring back at her from the mirror. She let Madame help her put the shoes on without taking her eyes off the mirror. The combination of the dress and matching tailored jacket gave her a sexy, sensuous shape that she had never seen before on her body.

"Hmm, stand up straight, belle. I need to hem." Madame instructed.

"How's it going in there?" Jonathan called out cheerfully.

Sam stiffened and her eyes flew to the doorway to the front room.

Madame's hands came to rest on her shoulders. "Cherie, relax. He will not come in. This is lady's place."

"Madame Vue, I don't think I can live up to this dress." Sam said hesitantly.

"Nonsense! You are perfect for this dress and it is perfect for you. I will give you to Adolfo to fix up your hair and makeup. We make appointment for Friday evening and you dress at Adolfo's." She went directly to the phone.

"Madame, wait!" Sam was waved off.

"Samantha, do you need my help?" Jonathan called out.

"No! Don't come in!" she called out frantically.

Madame Vue carried the cordless phone out into the front room to see Jonathan.

Resigned, Sam turned back to the mirror and gazed at her reflection. There was just no way to describe how she felt in this dress. It was almost like being Cinderella.

"Oui, oui. We finish the hem, now. Your man, he okays Adolfo without blinking. You are very special woman to him." Madame knelt on the floor and began pinning the dress.

"This just isn't me." Sam whispered.

"Non! I tell your Jonathan that you are princesa belle in this dress. He says non, you are princesa belle all the time." Madame tsked at her. "He will be sure to lose his heart to you in this dress, if he has not already." she murmured dreamily.

Sam blushed. "Are we finished here, Madame?"

"Oui." she helped Sam out of the jacket and then unzipped the dress for her.

It took Sam only a few minutes to change back into her own clothes and return to the front room.

"Hi." Jonathan stood as she entered the room. "How'd it go?"

"Fine."

"It was perfect." Madame Vue clucked and handed Sam a business card for Adolfo's salon. "You go to Adolfo at four thirty on Friday. I fix dress and bring it and shoes for you at five thirty." She turned to Jonathan. "You come get your belle dame at six and go to your party. If you can stand to share her!" she sang, pushing them out of the shop.

Sam stopped short on the sidewalk and turned to face Jonathan. "This is going to be too expensive. Let me pay for at least part of it."

He started to argue, but quickly changed his mind when he saw the stubborn look on her face. "We'll work something out, I promise."

Chapter Six

Sam worried about the party non-stop for the next two days. What if it was all a dream and the dress didn't fit? What if this Adolfo person burned her hair? What if she broke her heel or ripped her dress? She was preparing herself for the worst.

Jonathan offered to drive her to Adolfo's Friday afternoon, but she refused. She left work early to go home, let Molly out into the back yard for a while and to shower.

At four thirty she stood in front of Adolfo's salon with her purse clutched in front of her like a shield. Straightening her shoulders, she pushed her way into the shop. She was immediately greeted and shown to a private room.

A petite Spanish woman handed her a flowered house coat. "You leave on slip only." she instructed.

Sam nodded mutely and did as she was told. Moments later, someone knocked on the door.

"You are ready, yes?" a man called.

"Yes."

The door opened and a tall, skinny man entered the room. "Ah, Madame Vue said you were very beautiful. She was correct! Let me just get a look at your colors."

She stood patiently as he studied her next to several different color palettes.

"Yes, we have good colors for you. Please, sit and relax. Someone will come to shampoo your hair." he left quickly.

Almost immediately the door swung open and a woman entered. "All rightie! I'm Teresa and I'll be washing your hair and prepping it for Adolfo."

Sam sank into the chair in front of the shampoo sink and let the woman get to work.

When Adolfo returned a little while later, he was with yet another young woman.

"Melanie will do your nails and toes." he informed her. "Burgundy sunset. Very classy."

"Oh, but my shoes are closed-toe." Sam told them, hoping to shave some money off of the bill.

Melanie nudged her arm and grinned. "You never know what the night will bring. We'll just pamper those little piggies anyway."

Sam smiled wanly as Melanie rolled her stool into place and began working on her feet.

"Now," Adolfo announced, "we are going to make you elegant hair. I think we use pearl and diamond accents, yes. I will call Madame Vue and she will bring earrings to match."

Sam just sighed and closed her eyes. It was obviously out of her hands, so why should she bother to stress over it?

Adolfo was gentle with her hair, barely tugging at all. Melanie finished her toes quickly and moved to her hands. When Melanie left a while later, Adolfo clucked approvingly at the color on her nails. "Perfect for your coloring and a black-tie dinner."

"Mmm." Sam didn't even bother to open her eyes. She was so relaxed, it was almost comical.

"Here, just a little sweep there and we are done." he announced about twenty minutes later.

Sam opened her eyes but the mirror was behind her. "May I see?"

"Oh, no! You are a masterpiece in progress. You see final product only." he told her.

"Oh."

"We do makeup now. Where is that Tina?" he asked aloud.

"I'm here!" Tina rushed in with her makeup tray.

Sam took one look at the gum-popping teeny-bopper and groaned.

Adolfo laughed and patted her shoulder. "Not to worry, she is very good."

Tina grinned and popped her gum as Adolfo left the room. "Sorry, I came right from a class and didn't have time to clean up. Don't worry, I only do this," she indicated her face, "to me."

"I'm not worried."

"Good. Let's get going. Gee, you have great skin, especially for your coloring. I'm glad Adolfo went with the darker evening colors for you. Sometimes you have to fight him on that." She chattered on as she worked, powdering, smoothing, lining and curling. "I hear you have kind of an open neckline?"

Sam nodded. "It's a sweetheart neckline."

"I have this nice powder that gives your skin a very slight glitter. It's very light and it generally captivates the men." She laughed loudly. "You know how they like shiny things."

"Whatever you think." Sam shrugged.

"Oh boy, I like you!" Tina laughed again and reached for a container.

"Where is she?" came an accented voice.

"Uh oh, it's Madame Vue." Tina dusted the powder on quickly, her tongue stuck in her cheek. "It's about to get really crowded in here. You, my dear, look fabou. I am out." she grabbed her tray and scampered from the room.

Seconds later, Madame Vue came barreling in with an armful of things. "Adolfo is getting your dress from my car."

Sam waited patiently while Madame inspected her hair and makeup. "Is it all right?"

"You will see soon enough, cherie." she clucked.

Adolfo whisked in and out, leaving the dress behind.

"Let's get you into your hose, first." Madame instructed. "You will have to pull dress on from bottom so we don't mess perfect hair."

Sam followed her directions, then let Madame help with the zipper. The shoes followed and Madame stepped back to check the hem.

"Good. I bring earrings and necklace." she scrounged in one of her bags and found diamond and pearl droplet earrings. "These are just on loan tonight, princesa."

"They're beautiful." Sam carefully put them on as Madame put on, then arranged a silver and onyx necklace that complimented the neckline of the dress.

"Madame." A young woman poked her head into the room. "Jonathan is here. He says you are late."

Madame Vue sniffed and sent the woman away without responding. "Men, what do they know of beauty? It takes time, oui?"

Sam remained silent as Madame went through another bag. She held up a perfume bottle. "We put to your pulse points, cherie." she dabbed the rose-scented perfume on Sam's wrists, behind her earlobes, at the base of her throat, on the inside of her elbows and in the valley between her breasts. "That one just in case." she winked. "Let's get you in your jacket."

Sam put on the jacket and buttoned it while Madame unwrapped the last package.

"We will put your belongings in this pretty black clutch." She helped Sam transfer the major contents of her tan bag into the clutch. "Now, you are ready."

"May I see now?" Sam begged.

"Non! You will see yourself in your man's eyes first." She grabbed Sam's old purse in one hand and Sam's arm in the other. "Come."

"Jonathan!" Madame bellowed. "Your princesa is ready!"

"Finally! We're going to be la..." his voice trailed off as Sam appeared. His eyes widened and he felt like he had been sucker-punched in the stomach. "Samantha." he breathed, desire flaring up in his eyes. "You are the most gorgeous creature I have ever set my eyes on!"

Sam stared deep into his blue eyes and saw a raw hunger burning there. "Madame." she whispered. "Please."

Jonathan watched as Madame turned Samantha to face one of the salon's full-length mirrors.

Sam gasped out loud at the person staring back at her. That couldn't be her! Her hair was swept up high on her head, with wispy tendrils curling around her face. Diamond and pearl hair combs glittered from her dark hair, catching the earrings gracefully dangling from her ears. The dress was everything she remembered and more. It seemed to glide seductively over all of her curves, accenting her full bust, the dip at her waist and the flare of her hips. Tina's makeup was artfully applied and merely accented her naturally elegant features. As she stared at herself, Jonathan appeared behind her.

"You are like a dream. She was right, I don't want to share you at all." he whispered, his intense blue eyes meeting hers in the mirror.

"Adolfo, the camera." Madame demanded.

They took pictures first of the couple, and then several shots of just Sam.

"Go, go!" Madame pushed them from the shop. "You have much magic to make tonight!"

Jonathan was having trouble keeping his mind and his eyes on the road.

"You haven't said a word since we left Adolfo's." Sam said softly. "Is there something wrong?"

"Yes." he stated tersely.

Her heart dropped. "I'll pay for it all somehow, Jon. I didn't have any idea they would go this far."

"Samantha, forget about the money. The problem is that they spent all that time making you look so incredible and I want to spend no longer than thirty seconds ripping it all off and burying myself inside you." his voice was low and almost anguished.

"Oh."

He grinned at her. "I'm certain Madame Vue and Adolfo would both have me murdered for even *thinking* that."

Sam chuckled and thought about Madame's last perfume spot, 'just in case'. "Maybe."

"So, how do you feel in all that?"

"Well, I certainly feel pampered." she answered. "But I'm half afraid I'm going to break or that pieces of me might fall away during the evening."

Jonathan laughed and brought her hand to his lips for a kiss. "You'll hold together, I'm sure."

The hotel where the dinner was being held was a prestigious one. A valet rushed up to the car and took it away. Just inside the door, a hostess was instructing them where to go.

"This is lovely." Sam said, her hand resting in the crook of Jonathan's elbow. "And you," she whispered close to his ear, "look extremely dashing."

He turned his head quickly and caught her lips for a quick kiss. "It must be the angel lighting on my arm." he responded.

She blushed and let him lead her into the ballroom. "Will you know many people here?"

"Personally? Maybe twenty or so." he answered, smiling at someone he recognized. "Let's find our table, so you can set your purse down."

They found their place cards on a table in the corner across from the doors. Sam set her purse on the chair, then turned back to Jonathan.

"Would you like a drink? Maybe some champagne?" he offered.

"Are you going to have one?" she asked tentatively.

He hugged her to his side and grinned wryly. "I'm going to need something a little stronger than that."

Sam refused to let his comments bring her down. Tonight, she felt almost worthy of them. "Then I will have a glass of champagne."

"Good." They walked toward the bar, hips bumping and rubbing sensuously against one another. Halfway across the room, they were stopped by a man who was just separating from a group.

"Jonathan! How good to see you again!" he exclaimed.

"Barry, it's a pleasure." Jonathan shook his hand. "This is my beautiful companion, Samantha Velmar. Samantha, this is Barry Breader. We went to college together."

Samantha gave the blond-haired man a brilliant smile and put out her hand in greeting. To her delight, he grasped it and pressed a kiss to the back of it.

"The pleasure is all mine." Barry said smoothly.

Jonathan's gut tightened. Did she have to smile so sweetly at him? "We were just on our way to the bar."

"Hey, Jonathan, where have you been hiding this delicate flower?" he clapped Jonathan on the back.

Samantha grinned as Jonathan hugged her closer to him. "Jon has a problem with sharing, you know. And sometimes he fights with the other children." she teased.

Barry laughed and walked with them to the bar. "I guess you see a whole different side of *Jon* than the rest of us ever did."

She loosened her arm from Jonathan's waist as they stopped next to the bar. "Now why would you say something like that."

Jonathan stepped away and ordered their drinks, keeping one eye on them.

"To be frank, I've never seen him look quite so... content in a woman's company." he winked at her. "Usually he brings some female colleague to these things, then wanders off on his own."

Jonathan returned and handed Samantha her drink. "Telling tales out of school again, Barry?"

"Any chance I get, buddy."

Samantha leaned into Jonathan's side when he slung his arm around her shoulders. "Are you here alone, Barry?"

"Is that an interested inquiry or a subtle hint telling me to get lost?" he grinned.

"No lady likes to be deserted at a party." she scolded him before turning away and heading back to the table with Jonathan.

He pulled out her chair for her, then sat in the chair next to her. Reaching out, he wrapped a hand around the back of her neck and pulled her toward him for a quick, hard kiss. "I didn't like you talking to him."

She frowned and met his gaze. "Why?"

"It made me jealous." he grumbled. "And you smiled too much."

She rested her hand against his cheek and leaned very close. "My smile is just for you, Jon."

Groaning, he closed his eyes and rested his forehead against hers. "Don't do this to me."

"Do what?" she whispered.

"Jonathan!"

He jerked away from her and looked up. "Mrs. Farmer, how lovely to see you." he stood and pressed a kiss to her cheek. "How is your husband, doing?"

"Much better." the older woman patted his hand. "The bypass surgery was frightening, but he pulled through."

"That's great." he glanced down at Samantha. "Mrs. Farmer, this is my companion, Samantha Velmar. Samantha, this is Mrs. Farmer."

Sam shook her hand and smiled. "It's nice to meet you." She sat patiently while the two of them chatted briefly. Then she nodded a farewell before Mrs. Farmer departed.

Jonathan returned to his chair next to Samantha. "The Farmers have known my parents for a lot of years. Jim Farmer had a heart attack shortly before my dad died. I guess they only did the bypass recently."

"She seemed nice."

He smiled. "They're a nice couple. I'm sure to hear from my Mom tomorrow about my 'companion' at tonight's function." As he reached for his scotch glass, he felt one of her soft hands on his thigh. "Samantha."

She turned her gaze from the empty dance floor to his face. "Hmm?"

"What are you doing?"

"Wondering if there will be dancing after dinner." she responded, when in fact she was wondering what Mrs. Farmer would tell Jon's mother about her.

The thought of her soft, curvaceous body pressed intimately against his made him groan and still the hand on his leg. "I'm not sure my business persona could handle me mauling you at this particular dinner party."

"But I love dancing with you! I'm sure you would behave appropriately in front of all these people." she turned her palm up and clasped his hand in hers.

"I'm not so sure my body would behave. There are some things I can't tame, no matter where I am." he told her with a dangerous smile.

"Jon..."

A waiter appeared at her side with a tray of plates and began placing food in front of them.

"I ordered the prime rib for both of us. I hope that's all right." he released her hand and nodded to her plate.

"It's fine, but Jon..."

"I won't attack you while you're eating dinner, Samantha." he teased. "Breakfast, maybe, but not dinner." Without any further conversation, he reached for his napkin.

Sam ate slowly, wondering how she was going to wrestle an explanation from him. When she was finished with her meal, she excused herself and went to the ladies room.

As she was leaving the bathroom, she heard two women murmuring from the interior room. Bits and pieces of conversation reached her at the door.

"...you see that dress? It must have cost..."

"I can't believe it..."

"...he should have come alone instead of bringing..."

Laughter split the discussion and Sam left the room quickly. She couldn't be sure they were talking about her. There were a lot of women at the party and most of them were wearing expensive gowns.

Jonathan stood as she approached the table. He leaned close, asking, "Is everything all right?"

She nodded and sat down. As Jonathan sat, he took her hand but turned to continue his conversation. There was a cup of hot tea where her plate was earlier and she assumed Jon had ordered it for her. It was nice that he remembered her preference for tea over coffee. Reaching for the sugar, she started when the older woman on her left tapped her arm.

"Miss?"

Sam turned and smiled at her. "Yes?"

"I've been admiring your dress, dear."

"Oh, thank you." Sam spooned some sugar in her tea.

"May I ask where you got it?"

Sam's smile widened. "Madame Vue's..." she began.

"Ah, you know Madame Vue! Well," she turned away, "that would explain it."

Sam's face froze as she found herself staring at the back of her neighbor's gray-haired head, wondering just exactly what that meant. Feeling insecure, she scooted her chair closer to Jon's. She felt his hand rest on her thigh, indicating his awareness of her approach. Abandoning her tea, she leaned against his arm and tried to listen in on his conversation.

Jonathan smiled absently at the man next to him, nodding at something he said. The man could have been discussing a corporate takeover or a bake sale for as much as he was paying attention at the moment. All he could do was feel Samantha's breast pressing against his arm. Finally, he excused himself and turned back to Samantha. She smiled at him but he spotted a lingering sadness in her eyes. "Hi."

"Hi."

"Everything okay?" he touched her cheek.

"Of course. I didn't mean to interrupt your conversation." she said.

"I was having trouble concentrating." he murmured, brushing his fingers along her jaw.

"Why?"

"The blood in my brain went running for cover the minute you touched me." he whispered.

She frowned and whispered back, "Why do you say things like that?"

He blinked. "Because it's true. You wreak havoc with my body as well as my mind."

"You don't have to say those things." she stared at his coffee cup.

It was his turn to frown. "You don't believe me?"

"It doesn't matter."

"Of course it does." he whispered fiercely. "I don't say things I don't mean."

Her eyes flickered to his face. "I never said that."

"You just did." They were both speaking quietly so no one even noticed when he grabbed her hand in his. "Every time that I've said I'm turned on by you, this is what I mean." He slipped her hand over his thigh and under the table cloth. He could feel her hand trembling in his as he rested it on his hardened sex.

She sucked in her breath and her fingers involuntarily brushed along his length. Jon's hand tightened around her wrist before pushing her away.

Leaning forward, he placed his lips right next to her ear. "It's like I'm in a constant state of arousal when I'm near you."

She pressed her cheek against his and spoke very, very softly. "Please, I want to go home."

Chapter Seven

Jonathan sat back and looked into her eyes. There was a spark of desire there, mingled again with a sadness he didn't understand. "All right." He would never refuse her anything. Without speaking to anyone, he stood and helped her to her feet.

Sam picked up her purse and led them toward the door. She could feel Jonathan's hand pressed firmly against the small of her back.

Once outside, Jonathan handed his ticket to the valet and turned Samantha to face him. "You know what?"

"What?" she whispered.

"I changed my mind." he said, touching her throat where the moonlight sparkled back at him from her radiant skin.

"About what?"

"Thirty seconds would be too long to wait." He turned away as the valet pulled up in his car.

She stared at him for a moment before stepping toward the passenger door. She slid into the seat and the valet closed the door after her.

Jonathan got in on the driver's side and looked at her briefly before pulling the car away from the curb. Once at her house, he took her keys from her and unlocked her front door. "I'll go in and try to block Molly from jumping on you."

She thanked him and stepped into the house behind him. "I want to go and change before I ruin this beautiful dress."

He nodded and caught the brunt of Molly's attack as Samantha scurried down the hallway to her bedroom. "Wanna go out, Molly?" he lead her to the back door and let her out into the fenced back yard.

In the bedroom, Sam carefully stripped and hung the dress on the closet door. She peeled off her hose and her slip, then pulled on a pair of knit pants and a vee-necked tunic shirt. Just before she left the room, she took off the expensive earrings and the necklace. Looking at herself in the mirror, she felt like Cinderella at 12:01 a.m. With a sigh, she headed for the living room where she found Jonathan sitting on the sofa.

He stood as she approached. "Hi."

"Hi."

"I let Molly out." he waved at the back door.

"Thanks." She stood awkwardly next to the coffee table. "I, um, had a good time tonight."

He crossed to her in two strides, framed her face with his big hands and kissed her.

Sam's hands went to his waist to brace herself.

Jonathan was dying to push his hands through her hair, but it was still tucked tightly against her head. Instead he slid his hands along her throat and down to her arms. He pulled her closer, feeling the heat of her body warming his soul.

Sam felt his tongue tasting her lips and she opened her mouth to admit him. She heard him groan as their tongues met and sparred.

He flexed his hands on her arms, spreading his thumbs to brush against the side of her breasts. He felt her stiffen and withdraw almost immediately. "Samantha..."

She stepped back and out of his arms, trying to regulate her breathing. "I'm sorry, Jon."

It took him a minute to compose himself. "I didn't mean to push you."

Turning away, she wrapped her arms around herself. "It's not you."

He couldn't stand that she was so far away physically and emotionally. "Then tell me what it is. I want to help you get through it."

"Jon..."

"Samantha, whatever it is, I will understand." he said urgently.

"No, I don't think you can." she whispered.

"It wouldn't be for lack of trying, though. Just give me a clue, a hint?" he urged, stepping toward her. "I swear I won't judge you."

She turned back to him, but her lips were pressed tightly together.

"Are you afraid of me?"

She shook her head, anguish surrounding her in waves. "Never that."

"Are you afraid of a physical relationship between us?" he took one step closer. He could see her arms tighten around her. "Sam, you could never ever disappoint me in any way."

"You don't know that." she whispered. "I mean, look at me... *really look at me!*"

He stood silently for a moment, his eyes sweeping over her from head to toe. "I see you, Sam."

She shook her head, words from her past rising back to taunt her. "I don't think you do."

"I'm extremely attracted to you, as you are. Does that mean there's something wrong with me? My eyesight is damn near twenty-twenty, so I know exactly what I'm looking at." he said pointedly.

"I don't know."

"Has any man ever told you that you're beautiful, sexy and irresistible?" he asked her.

She held out a hand to stop him. "Please, don't..."

"Well?"

"No." There were tears in her voice.

He was close enough to touch her, but he didn't. "You're wrong. I have, over and over again. And I told you, I always mean what I say."

She shook her head, not wanting to listen.

"If you haven't heard me, how many other men haven't you heard?" he touched her shoulder lightly. "You are an incredibly beautiful and sexy woman and I find you absolutely irresistible." He looked her over again. "Unlike so many other women, you have breasts and hips, and enough curves to drive me insane!" he groaned and closed his eyes. "I lay awake at night, imagining what it will be like to discover every sexy inch of your body, from top to bottom. I want a woman who shouts that she is ALL woman and has the soft, sweet flesh to prove it. You are that woman, Samantha, and I want *you*. And nothing you ever do or say can or will change that."

"Jon," she whispered, "I'm afraid that when you touch me or see me without clothes on, you'll change your mind. I don't think I could bear that from you... You have no idea what clothing can hide."

"One of these days, you're going to let me prove you wrong. I dream about sinking myself deep inside you, and believe me, you're naked in my dreams." he teased gently. "Gloriously, incredibly naked, ripe and warm. Not every man wants a stick-thin woman. Famous painters drool over a body like yours. And so do I."

"I can't. Not yet."

He smiled when she used the word 'yet'. "I understand, honey. But I'm going to keep wearing you down, trust me." He gave her a quick peck on the lips and walked to the door. "Thank you for this glorious evening, Samantha." Then he was gone.

Sam locked the door behind him, then went to let Molly inside. His words were persuasive and lord how she longed to have his big body pressed against hers! She curled up on her bed under her covers, Molly's bulk a warm reassurance against her back. It didn't take much to remind her why this relationship would never be real, why she would never open herself to such pain. Closing her eyes, her parents' house appeared before her eyes.

"It's not that you're just another mouth to feed, Sammie..." her mother wrung her hands together.

"But you are." her step-father interrupted.

"And what with the babies eating solid food now." her mother referred to Sam's 18 year old sister's twins, living with the family, father unknown. "Well..."

"We can't afford ya no more." he grunted. "Frankly, we can feed them babies plenty easy if it wasn't for your big mouth."

Sam nodded and got to her feet, sixteen years of rage, anger and torment bubbling in the pit of her stomach. "You take care of those babies of yours, and you remember this moment for the rest of your life, because one day, I'm going to be successful, educated and happy. I'm the one person in this lousy house who has any chance of being someone! And I'll have a husband and family that loves me and supports me. You'll still have your 'babies' living with you, with *their* babies living with you, sucking you dry. My world will be far from here and far from you while yours will still be the same; hungry, dirty and poor. And when you come crawling to me for help, because you always do, I'll turn my back on you like you have done to me."

Her step-father snorted at her speech. "Ain't no man on this lord's green earth gonna love a pig like you. You may go and get yerself educated and get yerself some fancy job, but yer still gonna look like *that*." he poked a finger at her.

Sam heard her mouth gasp at his cruelty.

"Your words don't matter to me anymore. When you die, I'll dance on your grave." Without looking back, she walked out of the run-down house, past the sagging fence and onto the road. She never looked back, starting her own life in another state.

She never contacted or heard from her family in the eleven years since. Love was an unknown commodity in that house, and she felt no guilt at leaving them cold. Even though her mother had stayed home all the time with her own three children, and then with her daughter's twins, Sam had always been the odd child-out. She wasn't pretty like her older sister or the cherished only boy like her half-brother. She was the weird child who lived with her nose in a book, hidden away from the real world.

Becki was the oldest and spoiled rotten, which was why she was able to sneak out and sleep with every boy in town. Richard, her half-brother, was a slow-witted twelve year old when she left, and was probably still living at home. He showed early signs of taking after his father, tormenting Sam with cruel taunts about her weight and ungainliness. At sixteen, she graduated from high school early, taking classes through every summer, while still helping to support her family with a part-time job at the town's one major grocery store. And even with her store discount, they could never afford shopping there.

The phone broke through her tortured thoughts and she sniffled in the darkness. Wiping her face, she picked up the phone. "Hello?"

"Samantha?"

"Hi, Jon." She cleared her throat and said, "What's wrong?"

"I just wanted to tell you that I'll pick you up at ten thirty tomorrow morning to go pick up your car from Madame Vue's." he said quietly.

"Oh, I forgot about that. Make sure I remember to bring those beautiful earrings back to her." Sam requested.

"Samantha," he said softly into the phone, "I miss you."

She closed her eyes and imagined him next to her, whispering in her ear. "I miss you, too."

"I wish you were here, snuggled in my arms." he murmured, his voice low and warm. "I wish I were touching you right now."

She shivered under her covers as desire coiled in her stomach. "Jon..."

He groaned and whispered, "What I would give to hear you moan my name! To sink myself deep inside you and feel every quiver of your beautiful body."

"Don't..." she pleaded.

"Samantha, have you ever been with a man?" he asked softly, hating her answer no matter what it was.

Her breath hitched on a sob as she thought back to her short college career. "Yes." she whispered.

"Did he ever satisfy you?" he was torturing himself, but he needed to know.

"Jon..." The relationship had been relatively short-lived and far from satisfactory when it came to sex. She was convinced that the whole depressing period in her life was her fault, and was good reason to stay away from men. Her boyfriend, Mark, had sworn that he had a great sex life before her, and that his prolonged bouts of impotence were because of her appearance. The few times he had actually gotten an erection, the whole thing had lasted less than ten minutes. Shortly after, he had been off snoring or pulling on his clothes and sprinting out the door.

"Samantha, I'm going to make sure you writhe and moan in ecstasy every time you're in my arms." Her silent answer to his original question tore him apart. While he didn't relish competition in the form of an old boyfriend, it ripped him apart that some stupid man had abused her like that.

"I can't take this, Jon. You'd only grow to resent me..."

He could hear the tears clogging her throat. "Sam, don't do this to yourself. Whatever happened in the past will *not* repeat itself with us."

She wanted to believe him, but didn't think she could. "You're a wonderful and attractive man. You should have a woman who is your equal in every way."

"I already have that." He drew in a deep breath and tried to speak in a soothing voice. "I want to tell you something." He could feel his body tightening in anticipation. "Sometimes when I think of you touching me, I close my eyes and do it for you."

Her throat convulsed as she tried to swallow. "Jon..."

"Samantha, I want to touch you. Will you help me?" he asked.

"Oh lord..." she whispered.

"I promise I won't ask too much of you. Please, Samantha." he would have begged her if necessary.

"Okay."

He barely heard her soft-spoken acquiescence. "Oh, Sam..." he caught his breath and closed his eyes. "What are you wearing?"

"The same clothes as when you left." she told him.

"Will you take off your shirt?" He heard her shifting around and her soft affirmation. "And your bra? I want to touch your breasts." Once she indicated she had done so, he continued. "I bet your aureole is a light tan color, with a pinkish hue around the edges. And when the nipple hardens, it turns a darker brown and throbs in time with your heartbeat."

She was dying from the raw sexual desire in his voice. "Yes."

"Which hand is the phone in?" he asked huskily.

"My left."

"The first thing I'm going to do it cup your right breast in my hand. It's warm and tender and it swells into my palm. I can see the nipple pebble, yearning for my touch. I just can't disappoint it, so I roll it tenderly between my thumb and forefinger." He heard her catch her breath and his manhood hardened almost painfully. "Oh yeah, baby... does that make you ache for me?"

"Yes." she whispered.

"Pull on the nipple just a little, then cup your breast again." he instructed, trying to ignore the throbbing in his groin.

"Jon... please... I can't stand this..." she called to him.

He shuddered and remained silent for a moment. He could hear her ragged breathing over the line. "If I were there with you, my mouth and tongue would be all over your breasts, all over your body." he paused to draw in a deep breath. "And I'm not sure if I'd be able to stop."

"I've never felt like this before, Jon."

Her voice was so soft, he could barely hear her. "Like what, baby?"

"Like I'm going to die if I don't have you." Her breasts felt heavy and her nipples throbbed achingly. A pulse beat steadily and yearningly at the very core of her being.

He cursed softly and gripped the phone. "I won't let you die, honey. The solution to this is very easy and I promise it will happen."

He sighed. "I have got to get into a cold shower. Will you be all right? I hate to leave like this..."

"I'll be fine, I think."

"I could come over right now... it would only take me twenty minutes..." he offered.

"Oh, Jon..."

"Good night, Samantha. Have sweet dreams of me."

"Good night, Jon. See you at ten thirty." she murmured before hanging up the phone. Closing her eyes, she pulled the covers up over her bare breasts, sighing at the friction across her tender, aching nipples.

Chapter Eight

Sam threw open the front door, then faltered shyly under Jon's gaze.

"Good morning, gorgeous!" he greeted her brightly and gave her a chaste peck on the cheek. "Ready to go?"

She nodded and closed the door behind her. "How did you sleep?" she asked, then blushed furiously.

"Two cold showers later, I slept like a log." he grinned and held the car door open for her.

She slid into the car seat, then waited for him to get in behind the wheel. "I dreamt of you all night."

"Oh yeah? Was I good?"

She groaned. "It was all very innocent, you know. A little dancing, a moonlight stroll, that kind of thing."

"Ah, too bad." he smirked at her. "But we'll make up for it later, I promise."

"Jon, you're going the wrong way." she pointed out.

"Oh, I have to stop and pick up something from my mother's house for Madame Vue." he murmured absently.

"You what? Why didn't you warn me?!" she scolded him. "And here I am in an old pair of jeans and a raggedy tee shirt!"

Grinning, he patted her on the leg. "Honey, my mother doesn't stand on formalities like that." There was no way he was going to tell her that his mother had called at 8 a.m. that morning to grill him about his date. Without fail, Mrs. Farmer spilled the beans over the phone last night. While he had tried desperately to fend her off, she had overruled him and insisted they stop by this morning.

"Still, I wish you would have at least warned me." She flipped down the visor and checked her hair in the tiny mirror. "She's going to hate me!"

"Samantha, quit that! She's going to adore you, just like I do." he admonished, pulling into the asphalt driveway. "C'mon, let's go."

She got out of the car and let him take her hand. "I'm not very good with parents, Jon." She only had her own disastrous mother-daughter relationship to go by.

"Relax." Reaching out with his free hand, he pushed open the door and they stepped in. "Mom?"

"Come in, come in! I'm in the kitchen!" a voice called out.

Jonathan practically dragged Sam down the hallway toward the back of the house. They stepped into the light filled room. "Hi Mom." he leaned over the counter to kiss her smooth cheek.

"Good morning!" she sang. Quickly she dried her hands and came into the breakfast nook with them. "You must be Samantha."

Sam gave her a forced smile and shook her hand. Alaria's grip was confident and cool, her eyes friendly but assessing. "It's very nice to meet you, Mrs. Edwards."

Alaria smiled broadly and responded, "Please call me Alaria. It's an absolute pleasure to meet you! I've heard a lot about you."

Sam blushed and ducked her head.

"All good, I promise!" Alaria gestured to the polished wood kitchen table. "Do you have time to sit?"

"Sure." Jonathan answered for them, then pulled out chairs for both his mother and Samantha. Then he settled into the chair next to Sam.

"Jonathan tells me you work in a bookstore." Alaria began cheerfully. "Did you grow up around books?"

"Only in the local library." Sam responded, twining her fingers together nervously. "But I love them, old or new."

"I feel the same! New books have that tart smell to them and the paper is so crisp! Old books have the aura of history around them that is so intriguing." Alaria spouted.

Sam relaxed a little bit. "You should come in and see our Back Book Room. We have a lot of classic and antique items in there."

"Perhaps I will, if you'll promise to give me the personal tour."

"Of course, any time."

Alaria turned to Jonathan. "Tell me about the party last night. Madame Vue already promised me pictures of my handsome son and his exquisite lady-friend." She winked at Sam.

Jonathan grinned and sketched a quick picture of the night's activities. When he was finished, he stood. "We really need to get going. Where is that dress?"

They followed Alaria to the foyer where she pulled a dress in a plastic dress bag from a coat closet.

"You tell that Madame Vue this dress doesn't even cover my knees!" Alaria scoffed and shoved the dress into Jonathan's arms. "Samantha, you come back and visit any time."

Sam smiled and shook the woman's hand. "Don't forget to come and visit the bookstore."

"Deal." She kissed Jonathan's cheek, then waved them out the door. "Enjoy the day!"

Jonathan led Samantha back to the car.

"Are you going to tell Madame Vue what your mother said?" she asked.

"Hell no. I'm not an idiot." he grinned at her. "So, was that so bad?"

"She was nice." Sam said carefully. "A little intimidating." she admitted.

He frowned. "Is she all that different from your mother?"

"Oh yeah." was all she said.

Sam was engulfed in a hug the minute she went through Madame Vue's door. "Good morning, Madame."

Jonathan echoed the greeting from behind her, carrying the dress over his arm.

"You were quite the hit, yes?" Madame grinned happily.

Jonathan grinned back, then nudged Sam with his elbow. "Samantha was attracting stares all night. I was so jealous."

Samantha blushed and fumbled through her purse. "Madame, I brought your earrings and necklace back. I'd like to keep the purse, so just add it to my bill, please."

"Oui, no problem. You wait here. Jonathan, you bring Mama's dress." She led him off into the back room. "Here, give me the dress. Your Mama, she just doesn't like her knees."

Jonathan grinned and stood awkwardly in the brown and pink room. "She has perfect knees, just like everything else about her."

"Now," Madame placed her hands on her ample hips. "Your Mama says marriage comes to you soon, non?"

69

He blushed and looked away. "Maybe not all perfect. I believe she talks just a little too much."

"Non! She is right to say this to me. I want to make your Samantha's wedding dress." she stated bluntly. "But I must have six months to do it right."

"Six months?" Jonathan gulped. That cut his time to woo and win Samantha down to less than four months. And she was proving to be harder than he thought. There was so much more to learn about her and show her. "Six months? Couldn't you make it faster?" He almost slapped his hand over his mouth as soon as the words came out.

"Six months, oui. It will be beautiful dress. I start design on paper soon, but it is made by hand! It takes time and preparation." she pushed him toward the front room. "I am to be fourth to know of your proposal, Jonathan. You, your Samantha, your Mama, me!" she ticked off the numbers on her fingers.

"I'm sure my Mama will call you immediately." he said dryly.

Once back in the front room, Jonathan took Samantha by the arm. "Let's get your car."

"Samantha, your old purse. You left it at Adolfo's." Madame gave her the tan purse, then pushed them out the door. "I send your Mama extra pictures when they are ready, oui? For you both."

He nodded and ushered Sam to her car, his mind racing a million miles a minute. "I'll follow you home." he murmured, closing the driver's side door after her. He strode to his car and got in, slamming the door after him. Four measly little months... how was he going to pull it off?

Chapter Nine

"Tell me again, Simon, what happens if I don't meet the stipulations in my father's will?" Jonathan sighed tiredly and rubbed his eyes. He could hear the older man clear his throat before speaking into the phone.

"Well, if you don't meet the first stipulation, that is be married by your thirtieth birthday, the company will be sold and you will split the profits 50/50 with your mother. If you marry by your thirtieth, but fail to begin your family within a year, the company will go public and you'll retain only 49% control."

"What if it turns out that I *can't* have children?" He was looking everywhere for a loophole, but his father was always more experienced and more astute.

"If it is determined by an objective physician that you or your new bride cannot bear children, your father's will clearly states that you are not to be punished for this obstacle. You will split control of the company with your mother, and then your mother's will determines the company's future after her death." Simon cleared his throat again. "He's not trying to punish you, son. He's only trying to look out for your future as best he could."

"He didn't leave me any options, Simon. It was his way, or the highway."

"Now, now, only if you don't *try* does he really take the company away from you." he reminded Jonathan.

Snorting, Jonathan drummed his fingers on the desktop. "I have only a few months to find a suitable partner for the rest of my life and then..." he sat up straight in his chair. "What does the will say about divorce?"

There was reproach in the older man's voice. "Well, I'm almost sorry that you brought that up, Jonathan. It makes me wonder what you're really trying to do." When Jonathan made no attempt to defend himself, Simon continued. "If there is a divorce, ownership of the entire company reverts to your mother and it is up to her to decide its future."

"And there's no pulling a fast one over on her. If my marriage weren't true, she would never okay it in the first place." Running a hand through his already disheveled hair, he swivelled to look out the big picture window behind him. "Okay, Simon, that's all for now."

"I hear you're seeing a nice young lady. Perhaps she'll be the one...?"

"Good bye, Simon." Jonathan placed the receiver back in its cradle and gazed blankly out the window. Could he convince Samantha that she was in love with him? He already knew that his strong feelings for her would be a good start for a long-term relationship. The phone rang at his elbow and he frowned. Only his mother and Samantha had his private number and neither would call on it unless it was important. "Hello?"

"Hello, Jonathan."

He frowned at the tone of her voice. It was almost gleeful. "Hi, Mom." Simon couldn't have gotten to her so quickly. "What's going on?"

"I just wanted to tell you again what a lovely young woman I think Samantha is."

"I'm glad you like her."

"She would make a wonderful daughter-in-law." she prodded.

"I'm sure she'd be pleased you think that." his voice was neutral.

"Have the two of you discussed marriage yet?"

"No, we haven't."

"You haven't told her about the will, have you? Because no woman wants to think she's getting married for anything other than love." she instructed him.

"No, I haven't told her about the will."

"Good. You just keep charming her, sweetheart. There's no way she can turn you down." Alaria said proudly.

"You know, what Dad did was wrong." Jonathan blurted.

She sighed and responded softly, "I'm not sorry for what he did. You're much happier now that you've met Samantha."

"But Mom, the life of this company and the people who work for it depends on my personal relationship and it's future. That's wrong."

"You're a responsible and strong young man. You'll do what's right."

72

"But who's going to suffer, Mom?"

"Your father loved you and only wanted what was best for you," she said defensively.

"I only wish he would have talked this over with me. This goes beyond my personal life and I don't think he thought it through."

"You may not agree with what he did, but you'll see that it will work out perfectly in the end. I have faith in you just as I had absolute faith in your father." She brightened her voice. "Tell Samantha that I'll try to stop by the bookstore at the end of the week if she'll have time to see me."

"All right, Mom." He let her off the hook, knowing that no matter what he said, she couldn't change the facts and his words were only hurting her.

Samantha looked up as the bell over the door tinkled, announcing a visitor. It took her a moment to realize that it was really Jon's mother standing in her bookstore. Placing her stack of books on the counter on top of the inventory sheet, she approached the door.

"Samantha!" Alaria's smile was genuine.

"Hi! I'm glad you came." She was surprised and secretly a little pleased when Alaria leaned over and gave her a kiss on the cheek. "You picked a good day. Jon told me you're a big Hemingway fan, and we just got a signed copy of *Across the River and into the Trees* from an estate sale."

Alaria noted her use of the name 'Jon', but did not comment. "How exciting! Lead me to it!"

They walked toward the back of the store, then into a smaller room with several display cases and smaller shelves, anchored to the walls.

"Here it is." Sam led her to a table where the thick book sat closed. "We were amazed at the condition it was in. I knew as soon as Jon mentioned you were a buff, that this would be perfect for you."

"How sweet of you to think of me." Alaria gently opened the book and barely touched the spot where Hemingway's name was scrawled. "It really is an extraordinary piece. What price is it going for?"

Sam told her what the store paid for it at the estate sale. "We would only add ten percent to cover the processing, finder's fee and overhead. But that price is special just for you."

73

"Well, it certainly does pay to know the right person." Alaria reached out and squeezed Samantha's hand. "I'll take it."

"Wonderful!" She gathered the book up carefully and led Alaria out to the counter where the cash register sat. "Let me get a box to protect it." If they sold this book on the open market, Sam would stand to make a tidy commission on it. By selling it to Alaria, she gave up her commission and her only extra bonus came from actually finding it at the estate sale.

Alaria watched her tenderly wrap the book in bubblewrap before placing it in a hard cardboard box. "Samantha?"

"Yes?" she didn't look up, concentrating on securing the expensive book in the box.

"I want to thank you for what you've done for my son."

Startled brown eyes met sparkling blue ones. "What?"

"Since Jonathan has been seeing you, he's been so much more relaxed and much happier."

Samantha blushed and closed the box, sealing it with packing tape. "He's a wonderful man."

"He thinks the world of you." she paused. "I hope we have a chance to get to know each other better. I think we'll be good friends."

Taking her credit card, Sam rang up the purchase. "You and Jon are very close, aren't you?"

"Yes. I'm lucky that he always makes time for me. It was the same when his father was alive."

"That's a credit to you and your husband that Jon was brought up so well. I've never met such a warm, compassionate and caring person before." Sam told her.

"Why thank you!" She tucked her credit card back into her wallet. "Do you have a close relationship with your parents?"

"No, we aren't close."

Alaria blinked at the terse response, then continued as if they hadn't broached the subject of families. "I'm having a small lawn party this Sunday. I would love for you to come with Jonathan."

Lawn party? What did *that* mean? "Oh, okay. Can I bring something?"

Alaria picked up her package and touched Sam's hand gently, as if to apologize for her earlier question about her parents. "No, just bring yourself. Oh, and if you can drag that boy of mine along, that would be dandy." She winked and waved before leaving the store. Once outside, she frowned and walked to her car. What kind of childhood had Samantha had that made her so cold to her family? How sad that she had not been cherished as a miracle like Jonathan had been.

She wanted nothing more than to accept Samantha into her family and her arms so that the child could learn what a true family was all about. She was such a sweet and thoughtful woman, who could not love her?

Sam passed along the invitation that evening to Jon, who smiled and hugged her. "I'm glad the two of you are getting along."

She hated to show her ignorance, but it would be worse to be unprepared. "Jon, what *is* a lawn party?"

He watched her throw Molly's frisbee across the field. "It's like a barbeque, only the food isn't usually barbequed." When Molly blundered off after a butterfly, he sank down to the soft grass, tugging Sam down with him. "Don't worry, honey, it's very informal." If he knew his mother, this was probably a subtle attempt at introducing Samantha to her friends as her potential daughter-in-law. He kept that tidbit to himself.

Picking at the grass, one eye on Molly's whereabouts, she spoke to the ground. "Why would she invite me?"

"Well, first of all, she likes you. Secondly," he pressed a kiss to her neck, smiling as she squirmed away from him. "I like you."

"I'm really not very good at parties." she murmured.

"You'll be fine. And besides, I'll be there with you. We can protect each other."

"From what?" she raised an eyebrow at him.

He groaned. "She's going to start hinting about... things."

Her eyes widened. "What kind of things?"

Molly bounded over to them and tried to crawl onto Jonathan's lap. He grunted as she stepped none-too-delicately on his groin before giving up and flopping down next to Sam.

He adjusted his position and glared at the panting ball of fur. "Oh, you know, Mom-things. Like the future, marriage, kids."

"Oh." Those were 'Mom-things'?

It was his turn to stare at the ground. "How do you feel about those things, Samantha?"

She chewed her lip. "Is this a hypothetical question?"

"Sure."

She glanced over at him. He had responded just a little too quickly for her comfort. "Marriage is a fine institution for some people."

"What about for you?" he held his breath. Her eyes glazed over and he thought she wasn't going to answer.

"I didn't have a very good example of marriage when I was growing up." she said softly.

Taking her hand in his, he soothed her clenched fist open to press a kiss to the palm. "I'm sorry."

She gave him a wry smile. "Me, too." Sighing, she relaxed her hand in his. "I always wished it would have been like the books I read, but it wasn't. After a few years, I stopped wishing for it and started praying for a way out."

He sat silently, but did not release her hand.

"My dad died when I was little and my mother remarried soon after. She wasn't good at being alone and raising two little girls without any help was hard for her." her voice was taught with pain. "My step-father was a hard man and he never cared much for me. I don't really know why, not that it really matters."

"Do you still speak with them?"

Pressing her lips together, she tried to pull her hand from his. But it only made him hold tighter. "No."

"How long has it been?"

"Over eleven years." she said tonelessly.

It was hard for Jonathan to imagine not speaking with his family for over a decade. A thought so horrible struck him that he had to concentrate on not being sick. "Your step-father, did he ever... hurt you?"

"He never touched me."

He closed his eyes and said a silent prayer of thanks.

"He never even said one kind word to me. Not even when I lied about my age and got a job at twelve to help support the family." she whispered.

She grew up so young! Twelve years old and she was working to support a family who should have been supporting her. "Your mom...?"

"She was weak, Jon. She didn't know any other way to be."

"Did your step-father hit her?" he asked quietly.

"Not that I ever saw. But he was just mean. He screamed at her, beat her down emotionally and mentally. I hated hearing him call her awful names. And she just accepted it." She looked up at the sky and wiped at the tear that slipped from her eye.

"He yelled at you, too?" he guessed.

She laughed harshly. "When he lowered himself to speak to me at all."

What horrible things had that man said to her? Jonathan wanted to beat him to a pulp. "Do you have siblings?"

"An older sister and a younger half-brother."

"Do you speak with them?" he asked gently.

"No."

"You've been alone for eleven years, Samantha?" He couldn't imagine that loneliness.

"I've been alone all my life, Jon."

He gathered her into his arms. "Not anymore, my love."

She hugged him back, but her step-father's taunts still rang in her head.

GREAT LOVE

Chapter Ten

Sam pulled out her flowered spring-like dress for the lawn party. It had a tank-top style bodice, an elastic waist with a sash and a long flared skirt. She had a matching button-down sweater to wear over the top. Her casual tan sandals complimented the outfit.

When they arrived at Alaria's house, Jonathan bypassed the front door. "They'll all be in the back yard." he explained.

Nodding, she followed him around the side of the house.

He only hoped his mother would continue being diplomatic about his and Samantha's relationship. "There she is."

Sam tugged at her sweater as they wound their way over to where Alaria stood under an oak tree. The women and men scattered around the back yard were all dressed casually, but their clothing was a much higher class than her own discount special.

"Samantha, Jonathan!" She greeted them both with a hug and a kiss on the cheek. "I'm so glad you came."

"That you again for the invitation." Sam said timidly.

Alaria grasped her hand tightly. "What a lovely outfit! You have wonderful taste in clothes."

Smiling wanly, Sam plucked at the sweater. "Thank you."

"Lets go find you two some drinks." Alaria led them toward the buffet.

"You certainly have a pretty day for a party." Sam commented as Jon handed her a glass of punch.

"It's a beautiful afternoon." Alaria waved to someone who beckoned her from across the lawn. "Have something to eat." She gestured to the table before hurrying off.

Jonathan touched Sam's shoulder. "It's her first party since Dad passed away."

"Oh." She looked over to where Alaria stood with a small group of people. "She must miss him."

"Yeah."

She turned to him. "Do you have pictures of your dad?"

He blinked. "Sure. Want to see them?"

"I'd love to."

Taking her hand, he led her into the house through the sliding glass door in the kitchen. Inside, Jonathan first gave Sam a quick tour of the house.

"Did your parents want a big family?" she asked, gesturing to the bedrooms they just visited.

He led her back down the stairs to the family room. "I think so. But they waited so long to start a family..." he shrugged. "I guess they gave up after me."

Grinning, she swatted his arm. "Don't let it give you a fat head. They probably just didn't want to chance having another like you."

He reached out to grab her, but she eluded his grasp.

"Where are those pictures you promised me?" she asked sweetly.

He pointed to the fireplace. "There are a few up there."

She moved closer to inspect them. One of the pictures was of Alaria and a very handsome older man. Sam saw the resemblance right away. "Your father was very dashing."

"They were a good looking couple." he responded.

Nodding, she moved to study the next set of pictures. She giggled and looked over her shoulder at him. "You certainly were... cute."

He made a face at her as she studied the picture of him covered in mud after his first soccer game at seven years old. "Mom just loves that picture. I keep trying to hide it, but I think she has multiple copies." He looked over curiously when he heard her making soft choking noises. As he approached her side, he noticed the new picture she was gaping at.

"That's..."

"Us." he confirmed. The picture was one taken at Adolfo's the night of the black-tie affair. "I didn't know she got them from Madame already." He studied it for a moment, then slipped his arm around her shoulders. "We make a pretty nice couple ourselves, huh?"

She reached out and tentatively touched the wood frame as if she couldn't believe it were real. The couple in the picture looked too beautiful to be real people. And the look in Jon's eyes was pure, raw hunger. How could his mother display this where anyone could see it? "She can't leave this here." Sam blurted.

"What?"

Blinking, she looked at him as if he had just appeared out of nowhere. "Oh, ah, this spot should be for family. Like the rest of it." she waved at the other pictures.

He frowned. "Mom can pretty much decorate any way she chooses." Hugging her closer, he pressed a kiss to her temple. "Personally, I think it looks great right where it is."

The rest of the afternoon was pleasant for Sam. The food was good and the people she met seemed nice. They all accepted her as part of the crowd when Alaria paraded her around, introducing her with a proud smile as, 'Jonathan's lady-friend'. When the party began to draw to a close, Sam excused herself to go to the bathroom. On the way back out, she stopped to look at the picture again. She was just touching the glass when a voice came from behind her.

"It's a lovely picture."

"Oh!" Sam gasped in surprise and turned to find Alaria in the archway.

"I didn't mean to frighten you." she smiled.

"I didn't hear you come in." Sam said lamely, her hands clutched behind her back.

"The two of you look very happy together." her voice was almost wistful. She shook her head and gave Sam another bright smile. "Madame Vue sent copies for both you and Jonathan. Why don't you come with me to the den. They're on the desk."

Sam followed the graceful woman down the hall. "Thank you for inviting me to the party. I enjoyed it very much."

Alaria handed over a manilla envelop. "I'm pleased you were able to join us. Seeing my son with you is quite a treat."

"Oh?"

"Don't get me wrong, he's always a perfect gentleman. But with you, there's something more." she paused and looked Samantha over. "When you're next to him, he beams. When you're away from his side, his eyes constantly track your every move. It's like you're the sun and he's a flower looking for your nourishment." She pressed a hand to her flushed cheek. "It's like seeing myself when my husband Frank was alive."

Samantha didn't know what to say.

Alaria's soft gaze met hers. "It is a magical thing to see."

"There you are!" Jonathan exclaimed from the doorway. "Mom, your guests are looking for you."

She kissed his cheek. "I'm glad you both came. I'll talk with you soon, Jonathan." Turning back to Sam, she smiled. "Don't be a stranger, Samantha."

"Thank you again." Sam called after her retreating form.

"What were you girls up to?" he asked curiously.

"She gave me copies of the pictures from Madame." Sam said absently, still hearing Alaria's words in her head.

"Oh good. I almost forgot about them." he took the envelop from her and pulled out the pictures. "Hey, these are pretty good, Samantha."

She smiled and obediently looked over the pictures. In each, she studied Jon's expression closely, looking for the adoration Alaria alluded to. While he seemed intent on her, she wasn't sure she could pin as strong an emotion on him as his mother had painted.

Jonathan knew his time was running out. In order to relieve some of his own concerns, he contacted a local real estate agent named Rose Forsey.

"I'm looking to sell my apartment and buy a single family home." He declared out loud to his speaker phone.

"All right. What area did you want to move to?" the woman's voice was crisp and businesslike.

"I'd like to stay within half an hour of my office."

"Tell me what kind of house you're interested in?" she asked.

"I'd like to investigate any new home that would be available within the next six months or so. After that, I'd like to stick with houses up to four years old."

"What about size? Number of bedrooms and bathrooms? Are you looking for a large amount of property?"

"Oh." he paused. "Well, I guess I would like it to be fairly large. At least four bedrooms and two and a half bathrooms. I don't really know about property size... maybe half an acre or larger."

"Are you expecting to start a family?"

"Why?" he asked defensively.

"I thought you might want to receive information about the schools local to each area." she offered.

"Oh. You can do that?"

"Of course. Is there anything else you can think of that you want me to look for?"

"Not at the moment."

"Okay. I'd like to set up a time to come and see your apartment. In the meantime, I'll research prices for your place and put together a list of homes and neighborhoods to look at." she told him.

"I'm home most evenings after seven. Can we arrange an appointment in an evening?" he asked.

"Absolutely. If we can schedule it for, say, tomorrow evening, I can bring some information with me to show you." she offered.

"All right. Is eight o'clock too late?"

"That's fine. I look forward to meeting you and your wife."

He cleared his throat. "I'm not married."

"Oh. Well then I'll see you tomorrow evening."

Before she hung up, he passed along his exact address and phone numbers where he could be reached. Now, if only it were so easy with Samantha.

Jonathan had the dining room table cleared off by the time his agent arrived.

"Can I get you some coffee, Rose?" he offered after showing her the apartment.

"No, thank you. I've brought along some information about new developments in the areas you specified."

He smiled and motioned her toward the table. "We can spread everything out here."

"Good." She pulled a packet of papers from her briefcase. "I found four new neighborhoods for you to look at. Three of them are within half an hour of your office, the fourth is a little farther out but has more land available." She spread out the first brochure and pointed out the floor plan options. "In this particular home, you have your four bedrooms, two and a half bathrooms are standard, a full country kitchen, a separate dining room, living room, family room and den. You can have the basement finished with another room and full bath as well as a finished recreation room." Pulling out another glossy brochure, she indicated the picture. "This home is more of a farmhouse style, with a two-car garage and what they consider an in-law suite over the garage. That really only means an additional large bedroom with an attached private bathroom. This home in particular has three other bedrooms, two more bathrooms on the second floor as well as the powder room on the main floor. Then there's the standard country kitchen and breakfast nook, family room, living room, dining room and den. This style of house has a full wrap-around porch as well as the finished or unfinished basement. A fairly unique feature on the main floor is the mudroom between the garage and the kitchen where your washer and dryer are housed."

"What's the benefit to that?" he interrupted, studying the floor plan closely.

She laughed. "Actually, for a family with small children, it means being able to do the laundry without leaving the kids on another floor. Also, it makes the laundry closer to the dirt, i.e. snow clothes, muddy socks, etc. And another benefit is one less flight to lug the clothes up or down."

"And the drawbacks?"

"If it gets messy, it's more likely that other people will see it." She frowned. "But generally, the benefits outweigh the drawbacks. The other two new home developments are similar to the first. The farmhouse style homes are slightly farther away and generally start on three quarters of an acre plus."

"Are there many options available with that home?" he asked.

"Oh sure, they all offer different options, upgrades and add-ons. Depending on when you want to take possession, you can choose paint color, carpet color, cabinetry, fireplaces, decks, finished or partially finished basements and in some cases, upgraded master bathrooms and skylights." she listed.

"Are there models that we can look at?"

"Yes, each neighborhood has one or two finished models for viewing." she turned the brochure over to indicate the maps and hours listed.

"Do we need to make an appointment?"

"No, you can go any time they're open." She reached into her briefcase and handed him several of her business cards. "If you decide to go without me, give the representative my card to show that you already have an agent."

He accepted the cards and tucked them in his shirt pocket. "Do you have pricing on these homes?"

"Yes, each brochure has a pricing page tucked into it. I also brought along a compilation of the apartments that have sold in this building in the last year to give you an idea of what you may be able to ask." she pulled that list from her briefcase.

"How soon should I be putting it on the market if I want to be out in six months?"

She frowned. "I would say within the next two months at the latest. But it really does depend on the house you purchase and its actual delivery date."

"What can you tell me about each of these builders?"

She gave him an appreciating look and was glad that she thought to research that information. After filling him in as much as she could, she pointed out a listing on the back of one of the brochures. "The brochures list similar neighborhoods built by the same builder so you can compare."

"And you mentioned getting information on the local schools when we spoke on the phone." he prodded.

"Oh! Yes, I have that, too." More paper topped his growing stack. "I was able to find out about schools in each area from kindergarten to high school. I've included philosophies where applicable as well as teacher credentials and for the high school level, average SAT scores."

"Well, I appreciate your hard work. I'd like to look these brochures over." he stood.

"May I take a few pictures of your apartment so I can get started on an advertisement for it?" she asked.

"Oh, uh, sure. Is it clean enough?"

Smiling, she picked up her disposable camera and stood. "I'll only take pictures of the clean rooms."

After she left, he sat back down at the table to look at the brochures. He had to admit, the farmhouse was attractive to him. But looking at the location, he realized that his daily commute to work would be close to an hour. Sighing, he left the glossy advertisements on the table and went to call Samantha.

Chapter Eleven

Two Thursdays in a row, Jonathan received phone calls from Rose. She was encouraging him to put his apartment up soon because sales in his building of one bedroom units were slow. He expressed concern over selling too early and not having a place to live, but she indicated the sales contract could be contingent on the delivery date of his new home. She also suggested he speak with friends or family in the event that the new house's delivery date got pushed back.

After Rose's second call, he had Miss Patrick clear his Friday afternoon schedule. He wanted the time to investigate some of the neighborhoods listed on the brochures. He wasn't sure what he expected to find, but he was going to look at every angle.

After a relatively uneventful drive, he returned to his apartment to look at the brochures again. Maybe he would go out again on a weekend and speak with some of the homeowners. Not too many people were home at that time of day during a weekday.

He studied the brochures again, trying to envision himself in the houses pictured. Each neighborhood offered different facades and grades of land, but the floor plans within each community were similar. A visit was really in order to get the feel of the design of the homes.

The real problem was Samantha. Did he bring her and try to explain why he was looking at houses? How would he play that off without raising her suspicions or making her wary of his intentions? But then, could he really make a decision about what he hoped was *their* future without her input? Perhaps her taste in home features were different from his? This was going to take some real talent.

"You want to what?"

Jonathan fiddled with the salt shaker in the middle of the table. He decided that a public place would work best for this announcement. "I'm tired of living in the apartment. I envy the freedom you have in your house." *Good story!* "Plus, the market is great now and it would be a good investment."

She weighed his words carefully. "So what does this have to do with me?"

He blinked at her blunt question and was reprieved by the arrival of their food. When the waiter left, he answered her. "I want someone else's input and I value your opinion. I figured you were the perfect choice."

Frowning, she cut open her sweet potato and let the steam escape. "Why not your mother? She's done this before."

"My mother's taste is different from mine."

"And how do you know mine is similar?" she asked pointedly.

Uh oh. "Because you're an independent woman who has seen and experienced the world in ways my mother hasn't." *Good save!*

She still looked skeptical. "I don't know. It's still your decision what you do and don't want to spend your money on."

"Oh, absolutely. But like I said, I appreciate your insights and opinions."

"Hmm, how long should I let you continue to flatter me before I say okay?" she teased.

He looked up to meet her amused face. "What?"

"Now how could I say no to anything you ask of me?" she patted his hand before returning her attention to her plate. "So, have you told your mother about this potential move?"

"Not yet." It would only further her radical behavior about their relationship.

"What do you think she's going to say?" Sam asked innocently.

"I'm sure she'll be happy for me." Now *that* was an understatement. "She'll probably try to talk me into living in her neighborhood." he grinned.

"Would you do that?" there was curiosity in her voice.

"Nah. I love her, no question. But I want my own life, too."

"Well, its not as if you're moving out of state. So, tell me about the houses." she requested.

He was sketchy with his descriptions, saying he wanted her to get the full effect the next day.

The remainder of the evening went smoothly. They spent some quiet time at Sam's house, discussing the day's news and their respective work. After a short moonlit walk together around the neighborhood with Molly, Jon said his good night and went home.

They arrived at the closest development at ten, right when it opened. The woman there accepted Rose's card with a grunt and told them, "Feel free to wander."

Sam frowned, but followed Jon through the house. Upstairs she finally snagged his arm. "Saturdays should be one of their busiest days. Why then would they have someone like *that* to greet potential buyers?"

"Maybe she was mad that I'm already represented. That cuts her commission in half, doesn't it?"

"Hmph. An attitude like that gets her no commission at all. She's a salesperson and should accept *any* situation as a potential sale, whether it's a big one or a small one." she stated.

He gave her an appraising look. "So, what are you saying?"

"If this is the service you get on a sale, what is it going to be like after you've signed the papers? What if you run into problems during the building or just after settlement?" she asked. "This woman puts their whole business practice in question."

"And you wondered why I wanted you with me." he nudged her.

They bypassed the sales office by exiting through the front door instead of where the garage should have been.

The second development was a newer one. They only had two models and three out of twenty-seven homes built. And even then, the third home was a mere skeleton at the moment.

"Over-priced." Sam announced when they were back in his car.

"Explain." he instructed as he started the car.

"Okay, they had breakfast pastries and beverages out now, and will probably have snack foods later in the day. You're paying for that eventually. Also, they've been developing here for over a year and they barely have three homes built and only six total sold. That isn't a good sign. The saleswoman was pleasant, if a bit pushy, but the models were decorated with *real* things. Did you see the office in the den? All of the electronic equipment was real as were most of the other 'props', including all those books! If they do that in every community they're trying to sell, who do you think pays for that?" she released a breath. "Maybe you *should* consider a previously owned home."

"Don't panic, yet." he patted her hand, absorbing the logic in her statements. He had overlooked everything she noticed. Was it because he was too accustomed to the 'finer things' in life? "We still have two more places to visit." He was leaving his personal favorite for last.

Sam liked the next community and was impressed with the model. She pulled Jonathan into the master bedroom and pointed to the ceiling. "Cathedral ceilings." she sighed. "Very impractical for heating and cooling purposes, but so impressive!"

"So is that a plus or minus for this place?"

She grinned, ignoring his question, and did a little 'ta-dah!' in front of the fireplace across from the king-size bed. "What a luxury!"

Laughing, he followed her into the bathroom and exclaimed over the optional Jacuzzi. "For those grueling days of hard physical labor." he told her.

They made their way back downstairs and into the kitchen. There was a commercial sized refrigerator shown, an island, a double-oven, microwave, electric stove top, double-sink and a dishwasher. The whole kitchen opened into the breakfast nook, making it look large and airy. The formal living room showed another fireplace, the den sported built-in shelves and the family room had french doors leading out to the optional back deck.

"I like the quality of construction I've seen so far here." Jonathan said, comparing it to one of the other builders. "No obvious beams showing in the ceilings and no joint tape peeking through the wall paint."

They spoke briefly with the salesman, asking about community amenities and delivery dates.

"Well, our last stop for the afternoon is a little farther out." he told her.

"Doesn't that bother you?"

"I don't know yet. I guess I'd have to weigh it against the benefits, if any, that were offered." he answered.

"Could you work from home a couple of days a week, to save on some of the driving?" she suggested, settling comfortably onto the plush seat. "I'm assuming there's a den where you could set up your home office."

"That's an interesting idea. I know a lot of people are doing that these days. I wonder if it's cost effective enough to offer to our employees?" he thought aloud.

She laughed, poking him in the shoulder. "We're talking about you, for now."

He grinned as he drove along the interstate. "Sorry, my mind is forever running off with good ideas..."

"Why, thank you."

"And expounding on them."

She stuck her tongue out at him and looked out the window as they exited and headed for the development. She noted aloud that the homes were spread out nicely in the surrounding areas.

"That's a nice change."

"Just remember, *someone* is going to have to take care of all that property." she warned him.

He laughed and agreed. As he pulled up in front of one of the models, his heart soared. The stone exterior on the house was like nothing they had seen, and it gave the home a true farmhouse look.

They entered the house through the front door and were met in the two-story foyer by an older woman dressed in a comfortable skirt and sweater.

"Welcome, welcome. Come in!" she shook Sam's hand and introduced herself as Anne. "I'm glad you came. I'm only going to point out one thing and then you're welcome to take a look around the place."

Sam grinned at her Southern drawl.

"We haven't converted the garage in either model to preserve the look of the house. You will need to pardon the study, though, as that's where the office is instead." She waved them away. "Ya'll just give me a holler if you have questions."

"That means they won't have to redo the models before re-selling them." Sam whispered as they peered into the den through the double doors off the foyer. "Very practical."

The kitchen was bright and airy, with windows over the over-sized single bowl sink. There were all the same appliances as the previous house, except for the commercial fridge, set in honey-oak cabinetry and cream countertops. The island had a raised overhang and two stools for a breakfast bar. A peninsula separated off the breakfast nook that was complimented by a bay window. Off the breakfast nook they found the infamous mudroom leading out one door to the garage, and the other door onto the wraparound porch. There was also a big plastic laundry tub in the mudroom, that Sam pointed out to him. A back door between the peninsula and the bay window in the nook led out to the back deck. The dining room was off the other side of the kitchen. The living room sprawled off the end of the dining room through an archway and came around to meet the foyer. They found the powder room off the foyer near the door to the basement.

Upstairs they found the 'in-law' suite over the garage, with dormer windows that Sam squealed over. The other two bedrooms, adequately sized, were actually connected by a second bathroom, large enough to accommodate two teenagers. The master bedroom was huge, with sky lights in the cathedral ceiling and several double-high windows along one wall. There was even a large walk-in closet, but it was the bathroom that made Sam moan.

"Can you believe this?" she was practically drooling.

Double doors opened from the bedroom into a central area where there were two sinks in a single oversized vanity with a matching length mirror. To the left there was a single door leading into a moderate sized bathroom, with another sink and vanity, a commode and a full sized shower stall. To the right of the main area, there was another set of double doors leading to a room with a big step-up corner whirlpool tub. One side led up from the floor, the other led down into another clear glass-enclosed oversized shower stall with a big corner seat. There was a second door off the other side of the stall for entrance and exit at floor-level.

Jonathan came up behind her in the doorway. "Now this a room for entertaining!"

She grinned and waved at the skylights over the tub. "Talk about decadent!"

"The whole house is amazing."

"Can you imagine living in a place like this?" she whispered, eyes wide and dreamy.

His heart turned over and he knew he would cut off his right arm to buy this house for her. Emotions washed over him as he watched her wander back into the big bedroom. She bounced on the edge of the king-size bed and looked around. It was all so right! He strode to her, his steps never once faltering at what he was about to do. In a flash, he was on one knee before her and had her hand grasped in his. "Samantha..."

She looked into his eyes, then gasped. "Jon! What..."

"I love you. Will you marry me? Marry me and live with me in a beautiful house just like this!"

Her eyes glazed over and she thought she was going to faint. "W... what did you say?"

Grinning, he clasped her hand tighter in his. "Which part, honey? The marry me part or the house part?"

"You can't be serious?! This is a joke, right?" she whispered.

He pulled a blue velvet box from his pocket. "No joke, Samantha. I can't imagine living without you." He opened the box to reveal a moderate sized but startling pearl and diamond engagement ring. "Please, say yes."

She put her right hand on his cheek. "Oh, Jonathan..." Tears gathered in her eyes.

His heart constricted and he was suddenly afraid she was going to say no. "I understand if you need time." he whispered. "But will you wear the ring anyway?"

She held out her trembling left hand and let him slide the ring on. It fit perfectly and she gazed into his eyes lovingly. "I wouldn't accept this ring unless I were saying yes."

He looked from her, to the ring on her finger, then back to her again. "Then..."

"Yes! Oh yes!" She threw her arms around his neck and with them, threw away all her doubts and reservations. He loved her! She pressed kisses all over his face before his lips captured hers once and for all.

It was a few minutes before they scurried down the stairs to talk to Anne about delivery dates and available lots.

The three of them climbed into Anne's mini-van and toured the lots that would be ready for delivery in the next four to six months. They found one far back in the neighborhood that backed up to the woods bordering the community. The foundation was already poured and the outside walls were just starting to go up. Since the framework was barely in place, they would be able to select all their options except a walk-out basement, as the landscape would not permit it.

Anne accepted a small deposit, a mere sign of their intention to purchase, then sent them home with all the paperwork, sample sheets, brochures and pictures they could handle.

"You had this planned from the beginning, didn't you?"

He smiled sheepishly. "I wanted the house to be *ours* which is why I wanted you with me. I honestly didn't know I was going to propose until I was actually doing it."

"It was very romantic." she signed. "And G-rated enough to tell about in mixed company."

"Ah, the good old romantic but G-rated proposal. Every mother's dream." They laughed and held hands like teenagers, grinning stupidly at each other all the way home.

Chapter Twelve

Jonathan closed Sam's front door behind him and watched as she let Molly out into the back yard. This was going to become routine for them someday. When she turned back to face him, his heart skipped a beat. There was a happiness in her eyes he had never seen before. Without any words, she went straight into his arms.

"Oh, Jon, this is the best day of my entire life. I never dreamed anything like this would ever happen to me." she pressed her cheek against his shoulder.

He smiled into her hair. "You deserve to be happy. I'm going to make sure you're very happy for the rest of your life."

"You're everything I ever wanted. I didn't know men like you existed." she pulled back to look up into his face. "And since I didn't say it earlier, I want to say it now."

He raised his eyebrows in question.

"Jon, I love you, madly."

A grin split his face and he leaned over to press a kiss to her lips. "I don't believe I've ever heard anything sweeter in my life." Without waiting for her reply, he kissed her again. When he felt her melt into his arms, he knew it was all over. He didn't release her lips as he swept her into his arms. She murmured against his mouth, but he ignored her. It took no effort on his part to stride down the hall to her bedroom. The curtains were drawn against the sun so the room was dark and cool. As he neared the bed, he released her legs and let her slide to the floor along his body.

"Jon..." she was still marveling at his strength and the very romantic gesture.

"Shh..." he quieted her with a finger to her lips. Sweeping her hair over her shoulder, his lips found the spot where her neck met her shoulder. He heard her quick intake of breath, then felt her sigh. Her skin was smooth and sweet under his mouth and he moved slightly to her throat.

Fear made her timid, but it was the hot desire thrumming through her that made her tremble. She clutched at his shoulders and arched her neck to allow his lips full access to her sensitized flesh.

He returned to worship her lips, his big hands coming up to frame her face. "Samantha..." he whispered. It was killing him to keep his hands in neutral places, but he wasn't willing to jeopardize this moment for anything.

"Jon, please..."

"Please what, baby?" he whispered, rubbing his thumb across her swollen lower lip.

"I want..." she faltered and squeezed her eyes closed.

He pulled back and let his hands rest on her shoulders. "We aren't going to do anything unless you want us too." he promised.

She shuddered and leaned her forehead against his cheek. He was going to be her husband, her mate for life. To both of their surprise, she then pressed a kiss to the side of his neck, followed by a gentle suck on his jaw. She nibbled her way to his ear, her arms now wrapped around his waist. Her lips brushed his earlobe as she whispered, "I want you now."

He closed his eyes and groaned loudly. Her scent surrounded him and his body throbbed painfully at her closeness. "Are you sure? There's no pressure here, Samantha. I'm willing to wait." Air puffed across his ear a moment before he felt her suck his earlobe into her warm mouth. "Oh my..." his breath gushed out as she nibbled, then sucked harder.

Love was making her braver than she had ever been in her life. The hands at his waist began pulling his shirt from his pants. Though her fingers trembled, she smoothed them up along his muscular back.

"Samantha..." his voice was husky, but his hands were still on her shoulders.

She ignored him, letting her hands wander up his chest, pushing his shirt up and out of the way. When he still stood frozen, she bent over and pressed her lips to his right breastbone.

A droplet of sweat rolled down his temple and he nearly jumped out of his skin when her teeth grazed his right nipple. "That's it!" He released her shoulders and pushed his hands up along her ribcage. His hands literally ached to hold her, but instead he encountered a smooth barrier. That particular obstacle would be removed eventually, so he was willing to work with it for now. It was easy to find her nipples, which were jutting out from behind the cool material. He half expected her to stop him and was prepared to back off at her request. When she arched into his touch, he groaned and pushed her shirt up over her breasts.

She moaned as his hot mouth settled onto her cloth-covered breasts. There was no time to think about anything but his touch.

When he released her, he stopped to pull off his shirt, then hers. The room was still dark, but his eyes had adjusted enough so that he could see her. The white bra cradled her breasts snugly and without thinking he reached out to cup one breast.

Sam stood frozen, her eyes focused on his broad chest. Light curly hair was sprinkled sparingly over his pecs and led down to a triangle pointed to his zipper. He was beautiful and her hands itched to touch him. She blinked when he stepped forward and reached around her back.

"I have to see you. I have to know what you taste like." He moved slowly, treating her like a skittish colt.

Her eyes focused on his face, searching out his response. When she finally felt her bra fall away, she saw his gaze travel over her.

Before she could move to cover herself, he stepped forward and wrapped his arms around her. He shuddered at the feel of her soft fullness pressed against his chest. "You're beautiful. Even more so than I imagined."

She hugged him back, having only seen love shining from his eyes in the moments before they embraced. "You make me feel beautiful." she whispered.

When he pulled back, he was smiling at her in a sexy, drugged kind of way. "Let's lay down." He pulled her with him to the bed and settled down with her. He pushed her onto her back and leaned over her. As he kissed her, he cupped her breast, swallowing her gasp of pleasure. Her nipple poked at his palm and he responded by rolling it tenderly between his fingers.

She broke the kiss to pant and gulp air. He took the opportunity to lean over and pull her throbbing nipple into his mouth. Her hands automatically went to his head to pull him closer. Each tug of his mouth made her arch farther off the bed, toward him. She could feel liquid heat pooling between her thighs. "Jon..." she moaned as he transferred his attentions to her other breast.

He grunted but did not release her. Past experiences had prepared him for little response to his manipulations of her breasts. Most of the 'well-endowed' women he had been with claimed they had little sensation in their nipples or breasts. He was extremely pleased that she was enjoying this as he was a self-proclaimed 'breast-man'. When he sucked gently at a spot on the underside of her breast, she moaned loudly and twisted her torso so he could explore more easily.

Jon ran his hand over her stomach and let it come to rest on the button of her pants. Another part of her body that he was finding irresistible was the slightly rounded part of her stomach, just below her belly button. He didn't know what it was about that small portion of flesh, but his hand ran over it and settled there happily.

Moving one hand from his hair, she caressed his shoulder and back. "Jon, I'm not sure how long I can stand this."

He lifted his head and gazed at her, a smirk on his face. "Until we're done."

She met his smile with one of her own. It was a soft, dreamy smile that matched her eyes. "You're more than I expected."

Shrugging, he kissed her chin. "What can I say, I'm a giver." When her giggles slowed, he kissed her lips. "Actually, I believe I'm addicted to your breasts." he gently rubbed the sensitive underside and watch her eyes darken. "Yeah, right there." The urge to touch every part of her was rising. He rolled away and stood, then quickly shed his jeans and briefs.

Sam gasped, then clapped a hand to her mouth. She was nowhere near 'experienced,' but he looked huge! His manhood stood proudly from his body and she swallowed convulsively. "Oh, my." Her eyes met his. "You're very... um, large." she squeaked.

He smiled tenderly and approached her. "We'll go slowly." he promised.

She nodded, then sprang to her feet. "I'll be right back."

He watched avidly as she walked into the bathroom, then closed the door. He hoped she wouldn't take long, though he had no concerns about losing his erection. Desire throbbed through every part of him and he doubted that he would be completely satisfied even when they were finished. When she returned, she was clad only in a pair of pink underwear and her arms were crossed over her chest.

She scurried across the room and climbed under the covers, pulling the sheet up over her breasts.

Jon was not put off, but climbed under the covers with her. The sheets were cool against his skin as he slid over next to her. He pulled her into his embrace and held her for a moment. When she sighed and melted into his arms, he smiled. He let his hands begin their trip over her shoulders and arms. "Samantha, we need to talk about something first..."

She leaned her head back and looked at him. One of her hands began tracing his features. "Yes?"

"We should discuss birth control." he murmured, kissing her fingers when they brushed past his lips. "I want you to know some things. First, I've always been careful in the past and was checked about six months after my last, um, relationship. I don't want you to be worried about that."

"Thank you." she pressed a kiss to his jaw and let her hand drift down to his chest. "You don't have to worry, either."

"We should talk about kids..." he began.

She pushed herself up onto his chest, pressing her soft breasts against his hard planes. "Later."

Groaning, he sank his hands into her hair and pulled her down for a kiss.

Sam was encouraged by his urging and obvious physical response. She felt his hands at her breasts again and she moaned. He had incredible hands, plucking at her as if she were a favorite instrument.

He rolled her over onto her back, wedging his knee between her legs. His mouth devoured her, starting at her lips and trailing a path down to her panties. By now, he was completely beneath the covers and wouldn't be able to gauge her reaction to his advances. So, with a promise to himself to return, he made a similar return path to her breasts. He could see her face as his hand found the juncture of her thighs. Her eyes widened and her mouth formed a silent "O."

She lifted her hips and let him remove her underwear, then sighed as his hand cupped her. He was laying against her side, his manhood pressed against her hip. She could feel him throbbing and her own heartbeat matched his.

He held his breath, his cheek pressed against her collarbone, and dipped a finger inside her. He felt, rather than heard, her quick intake of breath. His finger slipped inside easily, finding her hot and wet. If it was possible, he grew harder. "I want you so badly."

Her legs closed around his hand as he sucked a nipple into his mouth. In her entire relationship with Bob, she had never felt like this. Not even if you summed up everything she ever felt in her physical relationship with Bob. "Jon..." she pulled his lips back to hers and rolled on her side to face him.

As he kissed her, he lifted her leg and draped it over his hip, pressing himself against her. He smoothed his hands over her back and down to cup her buttocks. "Sam..."

She arched her back, letting him guide her hips. As he thrust into her, she moaned his name aloud. "Jonathan!" She dug her heel into the small of his back, trying to pull him closer. He filled her up completely, touching her everywhere.

For just a moment, he lay still. She sheathed him like a glove, only tighter, hotter and wetter. He knew once and for all, that this was home for him. Capturing her lips again, they began to move together, each giving and taking equally.

It didn't take much effort to enjoy herself. Jon was a caring and sensitive lover, hers to touch and be touched by in this magical time. She could feel every inch of him sliding in and out of her. When he reached in between them to touch her, she gripped his shoulders and threw back her head.

He watched her toss her head back and forth, moaning and pressing herself against him. Her smooth throat was exposed to him and he leaned over to press kisses to her skin. "Oh, Samantha..." he murmured into her flesh. As he continued to stroke her, he could feel her tighten around him. It was only seconds later that she began to tremble and quiver, crying out and bucking her hips wildly. He removed his hand and grabbed her buttocks, thrusting madly with her. As the ripples inside her began to slow, he shifted his hips slightly and slowed his rhythm. Her response was a long, guttural moan and renewed ripples against his throbbing flesh. He groaned with her, then rolled her onto her back and started quickening his pace.

She squeezed her eyes shut and hung on to him, loving the feel of him on top of her. "Jon, oh my god!" she called out as waves of feelings washed over her for a second time. He stiffened over her, groaned and pumped his hips two more times before collapsing on top of her. She was trembling all over, her limbs weak. When he brushed her hair away from her face, she opened her eyes.

"Wow." he exhaled loudly.

She let out a huff of air and said with a grin, "Well, I never!"

He looked at her blankly for a minute, then burst into laughter. Hugging her tenderly, he laughed and pressed a kiss to her sweaty cheeks. "I'm only too happy to oblige, honey."

She lay underneath him, content to just be crushed under his weight. "I'll be sure to take you up on that. Again and again." she kissed his jaw.

After a few minutes, he rolled off of her and padded into the bathroom. When he returned, Sam scurried across the room and into the bathroom. She returned and practically dove across the room and under the covers. Curling into his arms, she rested her head on his chest and her hand on his stomach.

"This is nice." she sighed.

He hugged her closer, feeling her warmth at his side. "Yeah."

"Jon... will you stay tonight?" she whispered.

"I thought you'd never ask."

They lay quietly for a while and when Sam thought Jon had fallen asleep, she crawled out of bed and grabbed her robe. She pulled it on and walked down the hall to let Molly back into the house. Then she tiptoed back to the bedroom. There she found him sitting up against the headboard, the sheet pulled up to his waist.

"Oh! I thought you were asleep."

"Nope."

She stood awkwardly in the doorway, playing with the ties on her robe. "I, uh, had to let Molly into the house."

"And now you're coming back to bed."

She blushed and inched toward her side of the bed. "Yeah."

He threw back the covers for her. "Well, c'mon in honey, the water is fine."

Giggling, she slipped quickly out of her robe and under the covers next to him. "This has been just an incredible day."

He scooted down and curled himself around her back, spoon fashion. Crossing his arms over her chest, he cupped a breast in each hand. He felt her sigh. "Sam?"

"Mmm?"

"Honey, I'm sorry, but I didn't use... anything." he hugged her to him. "It felt so right to just slide in..."

Her face heated and she snuggled deeper into his embrace. "It's okay. I took care of it."

He blinked, not sure if he was disappointed or impressed. Then, another thought came to him. "It's, uh, still taken care of?"

"Yeah. Why?"

Grinning, he flipped her on her back. "Round two!"

"You couldn't possibly..." she felt him press against her thigh. "Oh."

"Don't underestimate this old guy." he teased.

Sam tried to roll over, only to find she couldn't move. Panicking, her eyes popped open to find a very masculine arm draped over her mid-section. She turned her head to find Jon stretched out on his stomach, his face turned toward her. He was adorable in sleep, a half-smile on his lips.

What is it going to be like to wake to him every morning? He had proved to be generous and thoughtful in every day life as well as their lovemaking. Would he be that way through their marriage and with their family? Gentle, caring and patient to a fault. She desperately wanted to think so. He would be a good and kind husband and father. Would she be able to live up to him and his expectations of her? As she sighed, he stirred beside her.

Jon didn't open his eyes, but reached up to cup her lush breast. It just seemed to call to him. "What a way to wake up."

"I can't think of any way that could be better." she murmured.

Groaning, he promised, "One day, I'll show you a better way."

"I'll look forward to it." She leaned toward him to accept a kiss. "You know, you have no clothes to change into."

"Maybe I'll just have to stay here in your bed." he pulled her closer and tucked his nose into the crook of her shoulder.

"Oh, what a horrible thought!"

He nipped at her neck and curved his hand around her flesh. "All right, I get the hint." Rolling away from her, he got to this feet and stretched.

She watched with interest as he padded unabashedly across the room, gathering his clothes along the way. His body was a feast for her eyes and she sighed unhappily as he disappeared into the bathroom.

A short time later, after Sam had showered and dressed, they drove together to Jon's apartment. He left her in the living room looking over his bookshelves while he went to shower and change.

Sam's fingers trailed over the spines of several books, her eyebrows raising at some of the titles. His classics were higher up, some of them duplicating her own collection. But on the shelves at eye-level there were dime-store westerns, mysteries, as well as non-fiction biographies. Business texts nestled in next to art history tomes and civil war collections. Then, stuffed in between some thick best sellers and books-made-into-movies, she found a slim hardback of poetry! It turned out to be an anthology of poems, some classic and some modern. What made her giggle and clap her hand over her mouth were the notes in the margins! His hand writing was far from neat, so she peered closely and squinted to try and read it.

"What are you doing?"

"Oh!" she jumped and dropped the book, her hand covering her pounding heart. "You scared me!"

He strode to her side and stooped down to retrieve the book from the floor.

"I was just looking at your books."

"And this is what you came up with?" he groaned and shoved it back onto the shelf haphazardly.

She giggled, then pressed her lips together to stifle her laughter.

"It was for a college course!" he protested, a blush creeping up his cheeks.

"Uh huh. So you kept it because...?"

"I paid good money for that thing!"

She snickered again and turned away from the bookshelf. "Whatever you say, darling."

He came up next to her and slid his arm around her waist. "I'm glad you feel that way, because I'd like to go tell Mom about us."

She stiffened, but he wouldn't release her from his embrace. "Oh?"

"She's going to be thrilled and will probably want to throw us an engagement party." he murmured, pressing kisses into the curve of her neck.

"A party?" she squeaked.

"I'll try to get her to keep it small, honey. But knowing her..."

"Jon, I'm just not good in party situations." she whispered.

"We'll stick together, I promise. And I'll try to make sure she keeps it casual. It's her way of showing her happiness for us." he soothed, rubbing her back gently.

"And the expense!"

"Don't worry, I'll keep her from going overboard."

She wrung her hands and stared at the floor. "I'm worried about having the kind of wedding she's going to want."

"We'll have the kind of wedding *we* want." he promised.

"I'm not going to be able to afford much... my savings is not huge and my family, well, is really out of the picture, you know."

He pulled her into his arms and kissed her forehead. "I'm not going to let you pay for this wedding all by yourself!"

"But traditionally, it's the woman's family who pays for the wedding." she pointed out.

"We're a modern couple and we're going to share everything. You're going to have the wedding you want and we'll take care of it together." he informed her.

"But what will your mother think?" she wailed.

"She doesn't care if you pay for it or if I pay for it. What's right in this situation is that we'll deal with it together."

She snuggled deeper into his arms, hiding her face in his chest. How can she go into this marriage so unequally? He was offering her the world, and she had nothing to give him. He was bringing his loving family, a stable business and a wonderfully caring upbringing. She was bringing a high school education and a mutt that he really wasn't too fond of. How was she going to pull this off?

Alaria squealed and pulled Samantha into her arms. "Welcome to the family!" She released Sam only to grab Jonathan and hug him. "This is wonderful news! You've made an old woman happy and given her a reason to live!"

"Mom, you're a long way from old, so stop that right now!" he grinned and propelled Sam down the hall to the family room where his mother was leading them.

"Tell me when this happened!" she settled onto the couch. "I want to hear everything."

Sam reluctantly sat on the couch while Jon took the chair near her. "It was all very romantic." she said tentatively.

He grinned and recapped yesterday afternoon's activities, including the house purchase. "I can't wait for you to see it, Mom."

She waved him away. "I'm sure it's lovely, but a house is just a house. It's the family that makes it a home. How exciting for you two! You'll have a new life together, in a new home with the future stretched out before you."

Sam stood and excused herself quietly to use the bathroom.

Alaria immediately scooted down the couch and whispered, "Have you told her anything?"

"No."

"Have you talked about children?"

His face tightened. "No."

Alaria was frowning when Sam came back into the room. "What's going on?"

Her face smoothed out instantly. "We were just wishing that Jonathan's father were here to celebrate with us. He would have adored you."

Somehow, Sam doubted that was the true topic of their conversation. "Oh."

"Come sit down, sweetheart." Alaria patted the cushion beside her. "Let's talk about the wedding and the engagement party!"

Jon groaned. "Mom, don't overdo this."

"Pish." she waved him away. "You're my only child and we're going to do this right."

Chapter Thirteen

"First, let us take measurements for your wedding dress. I'll get your drawings to choose from, oui? And then we look for clothes for your engagement party for Alaria." Madame Vue pointed for Samantha to stand in front of one of the mirrors.

"No, the engagement party is casual." Jon had been insisting for over a week that his mother was keeping the party small and informal.

"Mama-to-be calls me and tells me what she wants for the party. I find the bride-to-be something *more* spectacular." Madame began clucking around her, measuring and making notes on her sketch pad.

"I don't need anything for the engagement party." Sam protested again.

"You are guest of honor and you will look beautiful." Madame directed her to raise her arms. "Now, your wedding dress, let's look, oui." She led Sam to the couch and began laying out sketches on the coffee table. "What do you like? Traditional or modern? Long or short?"

Sam made a face at one of the designs that showed ruffles from top to bottom. "No ruffles." she stated emphatically.

Madame made a grunting noise and pushed the sketch aside. "You like this?"

Sam studied the traditional gown and its train. The bodice and arms were form-fitting with a high Victorian collar. The skirt was full and floor-length but the overall dress was relatively demure and almost... boring. "I don't think I want such a high neck, but I like the traditional look. And definitely no off-the-shoulder or sleeveless." she pushed away several other designs.

Frowning, Madame shuffled through the remaining sketches. "I don't know if I have anything traditional without high neck. The two go, oui?"

Sam stood and went to the mirror. "I want long, traditional but not flowery or prudish." she thought of Jon's fascination with her chest. "I want something vee-necked or with a sweetheart neckline that accentuates my bosom. A tight bodice that flares from the waist... even if I have to wear a steel corset."

Madame studied Samantha with a new eye. Who was this confident woman standing in her parlor? Everything she designed previously was for the Samantha she had met weeks before. "I will design for you. Don't you worry, non! I have picture in my head now. Your Jonathan, he wears tails, oui?"

"Well, he didn't say..." Sam turned back to Madame.

"You come back next Monday and I show you new designs. They will be perfect." Madame vowed.

"I want to be beautiful, Madame Vue. This is going to be a day to remember for the rest of my life." She stared at her reflection in the mirror a moment longer. "I don't want him to have any regrets."

"Yes, I have picture of you in my mind, now. Long train, delicate veils, long flowing skirts..." she stood and kissed the air near Sam's cheek. "I see you next week." Her eyes were dreamy as she walked away.

Sam gathered her purse and went out of the shop to her car. She was going to talk with Jon about the engagement party. Madame had been so engrossed with the new ideas for the dress, they hadn't even looked at outfits for the engagement party.

With mail in hand, Sam went into her house and dumped her purse on the kitchen table. She picked up the phone and dialed Jon's number at work. It rang only once.

"'Lo?"

"Hi, Jon." she murmured, accustomed to his absent answer on his private line. "I'm back from Madame's."

"Hi sweetheart. Did you pick out a sketch?"

Sam sifted through the mail, throwing out two advertisements along the way. "Not yet. But Jon, Madame Vue tried to get me to pick out an 'outfit' for the engagement party. Something nicer than your mother picked out. That isn't sounding very casual."

He sighed. "I'll talk to her. Did you pick anything out?" The tension over this party was all one-sided. His mother was having a great time planning it and barely noted his pleas to keep it simple. "Sam?" When she didn't respond, he called her name a little louder.

"Oh, what?" she looked at the phone as if it were a snake, a letter clasped in her other hand.

"Sam?"

She sat heavily at the kitchen table, the pale yellow stationary falling to the tabletop. "Jon..."

"Look, I promise I'll talk to Mom. You don't have to get a new outfit unless you want to."

New outfit? Were they really having a conversation about a *new outfit*? Words leapt from the page in front of her, choking off her air.

'My darling daughter, how I've missed you over these years.'

"Sam?!" he was nearly shouting into the phone now, thinking something had happened to her.

"I'm here." she whispered, her head resting in her hand, her eyes squeezed shut.

"What's wrong?"

"I got... a letter."

"Bad news, honey?"

She shuddered. "I don't know yet."

"Who's it from?"

"My mother."

For once in his almost thirty years of life, Jon was speechless.

"I have to go, Jon."

"What?" for a moment he thought she meant she was leaving town. Then he realized she needed space to absorb the letter. "Why don't you wait to read it until we're together, honey? You shouldn't have to read it alone."

"No, I need to, uh, face this on my own." She stood, barely realizing she was still on the phone. "I'm going to the park with Molly."

"Call me as soon as you get back." he requested, his concern for her evident in his voice.

She said goodbye and hung up. Molly was at her side after just one whistle. Then the two of them were out the door, the yellow pages tucked in Sam's pocket.

The park was filled with young mothers and their children. They were congregated near the tot lots, the little ones playing on the swings and in the sandbox. Sam led Molly up their favorite hill toward the open empty field along the jogging path. She let Molly off her leash and sat down in the soft grass. Smoothing out the papers on one leg, she swallowed and began reading.

> *'My darling daughter, how I've missed you over these years. I am sure this letter and these words will come as a surprise to you after such a long silence. I am writing to you to ask forgiveness of me for that horrible day so many years ago. When I let you go, I knew it was the best thing for you. I knew you were the strong one and would survive and even thrive away from us.*
>
> *I have tried to keep track of you and am proud of your accomplishments. I am sure you are a strong and independent woman -- everything I wanted for you and always wished I could be. I don't want to make excuses for the past -- I only want you to know that I never stopped loving you.*
>
> *It has been a while since I've heard about you and I am writing to beg you to come and see me. I want to see you as an adult, know you as a woman before I pass on to the next world. My Samantha, my child, I am dying and only hope to see you once more, to beg your forgiveness. So many things have changed and yet, so much has not. I don't want anything from you except the opportunity to say I love you again right to your beautiful face.*
>
> *Please, grant this dying woman her last wish. We have never moved and our phone number is the same. I beg you, please call, please come. I've made so many mistakes -- the ones I made with you haunt me every day of my life -- I want to make peace before my death.*
>
> *Your loving mother.'*

Sam closed her eyes, tears coursing down her cheeks. Dying. The date on the letter was just a week old, but how long had she known of her own demise? There was no mention of her illness or prognosis for her remaining life. With a jolt, she realized that poking through the pain of the past was a small ache at the thought of losing a parent.

But what about her step-father? Could she go back if he were still around? She never wanted to see *him* again! Was that selfish of her?

But how selfish had her mother been to send her away at only sixteen? To choose a man who beat her down over her own flesh and blood who loved her more than life?

Sam stood, calling Molly away from a nearby tree. The walk home only brought more questions. Her mother's handwriting was mere chicken scratch, but the language was what she remembered from her young childhood. Her mother had once been a well-educated school-teacher, but for less than a year. Then Becki had come along, followed soon after by her own birth.

Could she really forgive her mother? So many years had passed and so much bitterness rested in her heart... she just wasn't sure.

Walking back into her house, everything was the same, and yet it was all different. This was her chance to offer forgiveness to a dying woman, but there was no possibility of reclaiming her *mother*. It was a one-way situation. Could she put herself through that kind of pain for a woman who was basically a stranger to her in life -- and would remain as such into death? And what would Jon think of her if she rejected the woman who gave birth to her and was now begging for her kindness from her death-bed?

Sam was in the house only a few minutes before the phone rang. "Hello?"

"Are you okay?"

The concern in his voice washed over her, bringing the tears back to the surface. "I will be."

Jon let out a relieved breath. "What does she have to say?"

"She's... not well."

"I'm sorry, honey."

"She's asked me to come see her."

"That must be a hard decision for you. Whatever you decide to do, I'm here for you." he promised.

Sighing, she pushed her hand through her hair. "I don't know what to do, what to think, just yet."

"Do you want to talk about it?"

"It's been so many years. What would this change, really? Would it do anything more than open old wounds?"

"Maybe she's searching for closure on this particular wound?" he suggested.

"I'm not sure if I can give it to her." Sam whispered. "I'm not sure if I *can* forgive her."

"She hurt you." he said simply. "She should have been protecting you from that kind of pain, but she didn't."

"But did she have a choice?"

"I don't know, honey." his voice was soft but loving. "She's the only one who can answer that. Maybe seeing her would bring *you* some closure."

"I just don't know."

Sam tried avoiding the thoughts and questions surrounding her mother for several days. It was Friday afternoon when the subject was forced upon her. An overnight envelope arrived at her house, postmarked in her hometown. There was no return address and the writing on the cardboard envelop was not her mother's. Inside was a note on white lined paper with a small newspaper clipping stapled at the bottom. The note was brief, indicating that her mother had left instructions with the librarian, Sue, to forward the clipping when the time came. Sue was a school-time friend of her mother's and was the town librarian for as long as Sam could remember. Was that how her mother had kept track of her? Had Sue tracked her progress over the past decade and reported back to her mother?

The tiny newspaper clipping turned out to be a notice in the town's obituary section, announcing her mother's death on Wednesday. Sam barely had her mother's letter for two days by then. It wasn't her fault that her mother had died so soon! The funeral, the obit stated, was to be held Saturday afternoon at two-thirty, the burial immediately following.

"Samantha!"

"I'm in the kitchen." she called as Molly shot to her feet and bolted in the foyer.

Jon strode into the room and pressed a kiss to Sam's temple. "Been home long?" She was still dressed in her work clothes, seated at the table.

"Not really."

He pointed to the envelope with one hand while patting Molly's head with the other. "What's that?"

She handed him the paper, then stood and walked from the room.

He scanned the letter and obituary, then tracked her down in her bedroom. She was in the midst of changing her clothes as he leaned against the door frame. "I'm sorry."

She barely looked up.

"Do you want to go to the funeral?" he asked softly.

"What would be the point?" her voice was muffled through a sweater as she pulled it over her head.

"Just to pay your respects to the woman who gave birth to you and raised you for sixteen years." his voice was low but not accusing.

"The same woman who tossed me out of her home at an age where I should have been learning to trust the world." she reminded him.

She had let him read the letter from her mother. "She thought she was doing what was best. What if your step-father was abusing her? She would have wanted you to have a chance to live without that hanging over your head."

She sat on the edge of the bed. "How can I go back there? He'll be there, too."

Jon moved to her side, sliding a comforting arm around her shoulders. "I'll go with you and together we'll face whatever happens. Maybe you'll be able to find closure in her death."

Her head lolled on his shoulder. "We'll never get a plane out."

"You leave the details to me. I'll take care of everything." he told her softly.

They found a flight landing at eleven a.m. at the nearest airport, roughly ninety minutes from Sam's hometown. They both dressed for the funeral before boarding their nine a.m. takeoff. Having never flown before, Sam clung to Jon through the entire flight. He tried to entertain her and sidetrack her, but it was difficult. When they finally landed, he practically had to pry her hands from the armrest.

"I'm sorry I'm being such a baby." she said as they left the plane.

"Are you kidding? You did great for a first time flyer. The ride home will be easier, you'll see." he reassured her. Between the two of them, they had only brought a small carry-on bag with emergency items for the day. Their return flight was scheduled to leave at ten p.m. that night.

As they walked through the airport holding hands, Jon scanned the waiting area near the front doors.

"Don't we need to rent a car?" she asked, tugging him toward the rental stands.

"Nope." He finally spotted the person he was looking for. "This way."

She followed him toward a man in a dark suit holding a sign with 'J. Edwards' printed on it. "Jon... what... ?"

"I'm Jon Edwards." he announced.

"Yes, sir. I'm your driver, Michael." he took the overnight bag from Jon. "Do you have any other bags?"

"No, that's it." Jon answered.

"The car is right out front." he led them to a dark gray limo.

"Jon." she hissed, tugging at his hand. "What *is* this?"

He turned as the driver opened the back door for them. "I hired a limo so we didn't have to worry about the drive."

"But Jon..."

He pushed her gently into the car, then followed. "Honey, it's going to be a long day. This way we don't have to worry about being tired later tonight for the drive back."

"We could have taken a cab."

"This was cheaper, trust me." he grinned and settled back onto the plush seats. "Driver!" he called.

"Yes, sir?"

"We'd like to stop somewhere for a quick bite to eat before going to the funeral. Could you find someplace for us?" Jon requested.

"Of course, sir. What time would you like to eat?"

"Around noon would be fine." Jon answered before pulling Sam close to him and speaking to her softly. "Relax, it's going to be fine."

Lunch was a short affair at a clean, if somewhat old diner just off the highway. Sam ate little, her stomach in knots over the upcoming event. Burying a parent was supposed to be traumatic... why did she feel so numb? Jon was being sweet and supportive the whole ride, talking when she talked, silent when she ran out of things to say.

"We have some time before the funeral." Jon said softly as they entered the little town. "Is there anywhere you want to go or anything you want to see?"

"No. Could we just go to the funeral home? Maybe I could go in early and see if she's... maybe I could see her alone for a moment."

"Okay." He directed the chauffeur to go right to the funeral home.

When they pulled up in front of the small white building almost thirty minutes early, the lot was almost empty.

Sam and Jon walked through the front door, hand in hand. A young woman met them just inside the doors.

"Are you with the Jerman funeral?" she asked without greeting them.

"Yes." Sam answered, acknowledging her step-father's surname.

"It starts at two." came the curt response.

"I was hoping I could see her for a moment..." Sam began.

The young woman stared at her hard. "And you are?"

"I'm her daughter."

She looked taken aback. "Oh, well, then I suppose it's all right." She led them to a set of double doors. "Right through here. People will be arriving in about fifteen or twenty minutes for sure."

Sam straightened her shoulders and walked through the doors. She heard Jon follow hesitantly and remembered that it wasn't so long ago that he buried a parent as well. But she didn't feel near the torment she was sure he had for his loss.

And then, there it was. The plain coffin sat silently at the front of the room, seeming to loom larger than life. As she approached, her knees seemed to weaken and she reached out to steady herself. Instead of grasping the back of a pew, it was Jonathan's arm that steadied her. She gave him a small but grateful smile.

Together they walked up to the casket.

Sam stared down at the face of the woman who was at once familiar and yet not. It was definitely her, but age and a hard life had creased her skin and grayed her hair, leaving her looking beaten and sad.

"Oh, Mom." Sam whispered, her hand hovering over a wrinkled cheek.

Jon held Samantha close, not sure if she was going to burst into tears or walk away dry-eyed. He wasn't sure if she knew, either. "Honey, I'm sure she knows you came as soon as you could."

"I'm not sure it matters now for her."

They stepped away and found seats in one of the back pews as a few other people entered the room. Sam recognized a few, but others were strangers to her.

Just before two-thirty, the doors swung open and several people literally tumbled through. Sam had to stop herself from gasping out loud.

Jon looked up as Sam's fingers bit into his hand. A big, rotund, bearded man wearing pressed overalls led a pack of younger people toward the front pew. Right at his heels was a smaller, younger version of himself without the beard, that Jon assumed was his son and Sam's half-brother. Behind him was a woman dressed in a long, dark and unattractive dress dragging several children along. The older ones must be the twins, he thought, just in their teen years? Both were dressed in jeans and pressed white shirts bearing a few bleached-out stains. Then there were three other children in various stages of dress and age who plodded their way down the aisle.

"Oh Becki." Sam murmured quietly. If only the poor woman had had a father's love as a child, would she have avoided her rampage of men and the resulting children?

The funeral director stepped forward after the family settled into their pew. He addressed the small group of people, thanking them on behalf of the family, for attending.

The service was short and uninspired. Neither her mother nor her step-father had been particularly religious people, so they avoided a religious service all together. Not once during the entire service did any of the people in the front pew look around them. The children had to be shushed several times and once Becki had to get up to retrieve a youngster.

When the service was over, her step-father and half-brother stood and marched from the room without looking back. Becki took longer to gather up the children and when she turned, her eyes collided with Sam's.

Sam almost gasped. Becki looked exactly like she remembered her mother had looked eleven years ago. Her face was tired and drawn and lacked any spark of life. She scooped up a toddler and herded the group toward the back of the room. At their pew, she stopped and turned to face them.

"Samantha."

Tears filled Sam's eyes, but she controlled herself. "Becki."

The child in Becki's arms began to fidget. "You look well." her eyes flickered over Jon briefly.

"Thank you." Sam wasn't sure what to say. "Could we, uh, talk later?"

Becki frowned and shifted the baby in her arms. "I don't know if I'll have time." she said flatly.

Sam nodded silently and watched the brood leave. She and Jon followed them out. They walked to their waiting limo and got in as Becki was piling her family into an aged and beaten station wagon.

The drive to the cemetery took about twenty minutes. When they arrived, there were only a few cars there. Sam and Jon were approaching the gravesite when someone called Sam's name.

She turned to see the aging librarian coming toward them. "Hello, Sue."

The older woman smiled and hugged Samantha. "It's good to see you again."

"Thank you. How are you?" Sam asked politely.

"Good, thanks. Your mom would be happy that you were able to come." Sue walked with them toward the gravesite.

Sam remained silent, her hand tucked tightly in Jon's.

"She missed you. Used to come and reminisce with me at the library about you." Sue went on as they halted at the freshly dug hole in the ground.

Sam stared across the gravesite at the people who where once her family. Her step-father stood with Richard while Becki and her kids stood behind them. Just as it had always been. They stood dry-eyed as the funeral director spoke briefly. They never blinked as the coffin was lowered into the ground. Sue cried quietly at Sam's side the whole time.

The funeral director shook her step-father's hand, then walked away, his duty complete.

Sam stood frozen as her step-father met her gaze. Anger and resentment still shone brightly as if eleven years had not passed at all. Without a word, he turned and lumbered away, Richard at his heels. Sam was left gazing at her sister, whose eyes were riveted to the coffin in the ground.

"Will you have time to visit, Samantha?" Sue asked at her side.

"I don't know yet." Sam responded.

"Well, I'll be at Chuck's diner 'round five thirty for dinner if you want to join me." she murmured before moving away. She spoke with Becki before walking back to her own car.

Becki pushed her children toward the station wagon then strode toward Sam. "Guess you sure came back in style. Wondered who belonged to that limo. Thought for a minute it belonged to us mourners." She frowned and threw a glance at her car. "Guess you hafta go?"

"We have some time before our flight..." Sam began.

"You'd hafta come to the house." She stuck out her chin. "I got the kids to watch."

Sam's face tightened.

"They won't be there. Never are 'cept to sleep. They'll be off drinkin' now." Becki told her bluntly.

"Okay, we'll follow you." Once back in the limo, she turned to Jon. "I'm sorry, I should have checked with you before..."

He silenced her with a light kiss. "Nonsense. I'm here to support you, honey. Whatever you say, goes."

She sighed and leaned into his side. "Thank you for taking care of everything today."

He just hugged her as the limo followed the station wagon out of town. Too bad old papa-bear wasn't going to be around. Jonathan would have loved to get a punch in with the old bastard.

The limo slid to a stop in front of a small house with a sagging front porch.

"Home sweet home." Sam murmured.

"Ya'll go inside and get out of yer good clothes before you get 'em all dirty." Becki was yelling as they joined her on the porch. Then she turned to face Sam. "You want somethin' to drink?"

"Sure." Sam nodded. "Whatever you have that's cold."

"Make that two, please." Jon requested smoothly.

Becki returned with three glasses of iced tea. After handing off two glasses to her seated guests, she lowered herself to a chair. They were all silent for a few minutes.

"Tell me about your kids." Sam asked finally.

Becki frowned and eyed her warily. "You don't really care. You ain't gonna stay here and you ain't really a part of this family. Why *did* you come back?"

Sam put down her glass and turned to look at her sister. "Mom wrote to me. She asked me to come see her."

"So why didn't you?"

"I only got the letter on Monday. She never said how sick she was so I didn't know..." Sam trailed off.

"And before that?"

"She never wrote." Sam said.

"Neither did you."

"She sent me away." Sam defended herself.

"So you wouldn't end up like her or like me. And lookit yerself now." Becki poked a finger at her. "And never once did you call or write to say thank you."

"Thank you!" Sam gasped, wide-eyed. "I had to go survive on my own, alone, at sixteen! She let him kick me out and never once said she was sorry!"

Becki shook her head. "You don't get it! You were the one who had a chance. If she hadn't sent you out on your own, she would have had to watch you die slowly out here. Like me."

"What are you talking about?" Sam was confused.

"Sam, wake up!" Becki turned her head away to stare out at the road. "I knew exactly who the father of them twins were."

"Then why didn't you go with him and get out of here?"

"Cause it was *him*." Becki whispered.

"Joe?!" Sam asked incredulously.

Becki nodded at their step-father's name. "Raped me at sixteen."

Sam moaned and covered her face. "And for how long before that, Becki?"

Becki glanced self-consciously at Jon before answering. "Coupla years."

"And yet, you stayed." she whispered.

"Mom didn't believe me 'til after them babies was born. But they ended up looking just like Richard when he was a baby. And by then, I didn't have nowhere to go." Becki responded.

"And he wouldn't let you give them away?"

"He threatened me, Sam. Said he'd kill me if I tried." she wrung her hands together. ·

Sam cried out at the familiar gesture. Becki looked so much like their mother it hurt. "And the other children?" She was almost afraid to ask.

"No, they belong to other boys."

"Becki," Sam went to kneel in front of her old sister, "come back with me."

Becki blinked. "What?"

"You, the kids, come back with me. Get away from Joe. With Mom gone, there's no reason to stay and every reason to go."

Becki looked almost hopeful for a moment, then her shoulders fell. "I can't leave. I don't know any other way to be."

"I can help you." Sam took her hand. "We can put you in a house, find you a job..."

Becki shook her head. "Can't."

Sighing, Sam stood and turned to Jon. "We should go." Before they walked away, she turned back and pressed the bookstore's business card into Becki's hand. "If you change your mind, or if you need me..."

Nodding, Becki took the card, then watched them get into the limo and drive away.

Sam buried her head in Jon's shoulder and cried. "How could I have not seen?" she wailed.

He stroked her hair. "You were just a child. Why would you have any reason to see these things?"

"How many years did she suffer through that horrible man touching her?" she raged. "I have to get her out of there. With Mom gone, I'm positive he'll turn back to her."

"Honey, you can't kidnap her. If she doesn't want to go..."

"You heard her, she doesn't know any other way to be. I can help her find it! I'll just have to keep working on her. I'll have to find a way to convince her." she vowed. "I won't leave her to suffer alone again. I know what that's like... no one should have to live that way."

Chapter Fourteen

It was a Saturday, mid-morning, when Sam stumbled upon a scene that made her heart fill with joy. It was a rainy, dreary day so they had slept in and when they woke, Jon went to find some breakfast while she jumped in the shower. She was wrapped in a dark blue robe, toweling her hair as she padded quietly down the hall. As she came to the end of the hallway, she found Jon in her living room. He was wearing a pair of gray sweat pants and a white tee-shirt and was on the floor, wrestling with Molly! The two of them were rolling around on the floor, Molly's tail wagging enthusiastically as she pawed at Jon's arm and stumbled over his leg. Jon tugged at her floppy ears, scratched at her furry chest and ducked away from her lolling tongue. Sam smiled as he laughed and rolled away from Molly's oversized paw when she swiped at him again.

"You're just a big baby, aren't you?" he teased the mutt as she rolled onto her back to get her stomach scratched. "A real mama's dog, huh?" Grinning, he scratched her stomach and watched her wriggle in delight, tongue hanging out the side of her mouth. "And you definitely need a breath mint."

Sam stifled a giggle and stepped farther back into the shadows of the hallway.

"Too bad it's raining today, huh? No frisbee for Molly."

Sam clapped a hand over her mouth as Molly scrambled to her feet and rushed from the room. He should know by now how Molly would react to the sound of her toy's name. A second later, the mutt returned and dropped the red disc in his lap. She barked insistently at him.

"It's raining, you dumb dog." he laughed as she danced around him and nosed at the frisbee. "You want to go out and see for yourself, mutt?"

Molly barked and headed for the front door, thinking they were off for the park. She screeched to a halt and bolted to Sam's side the minute she spotted her lurking in the hallway.

"Busted." Sam laughed and stepped out into view, Molly jumping around her.

Jon stared at her for a moment, then a grin split his face. "I think I'm the one who's busted here. Exactly how much of that did you see?"

"Enough to know that you don't really hate 'the beast'." she grinned back.

He rolled lithely to his feet and walked toward her. "Think of the embarrassment you could have saved me if you had just let me shower with you."

"But think of your ultimate embarrassment in there." she teased him as he kissed her cheek.

"Oh, you wound me, love. I'm more than happy to prove you wrong." he tugged her hand toward the bedroom.

"It may take a while." she resisted playfully, letting him pull her down the hall.

"I'm definitely up for it."

They finally made it to the kitchen in time for lunch. Outside, the rain continued to fall and the sky remained dark.

"Maybe today would be a good day to look at our color options for the house." Sam suggested after lunch. "I just have to haul the stuff out of the spare room."

"I hate that stuff! It's even haunting me in my dreams." Jon protested.

"All the more reason to get it over with. And I am not," she held up her hand to ward him off. "making these decisions without you. You have to live there, too."

"But it doesn't matter to me what color the carpet is."

She ignored him and stood to fetch the swatches and samples from the bedroom. It only took one trip and she spread everything out on the living room floor. "Jon! C'mon, let's get this over with." she let Molly lay down at her side, then petted her head.

He whined all the way from the kitchen to the living room. "Just make everything black."

She pulled him down to the floor and spread out the paint samples. "Okay, beige or..." she picked up two samples and held them out. "...beige."

Grunting, he sifted through some samples. "Are they going to paint the whole house the same color?"

"Yeah, unless we want to pay the extra fees for different colors in different rooms."

"Hmph. Guess we should stick with something neutral, then. We can always repaint some rooms later." He was thinking about the decor needs for a nursery.

"That's true. So this part should be easy. Beige or gray." Pushing the paint samples around, she found a light beige and a light dove gray.

"I can't picture a gray kitchen, can you?"

She frowned and pulled out the board with the options for the kitchen cabinets and countertops. "I much prefer wood cabinets than a formica covering. It'll suit the country kitchen design."

"That's fine with me."

Holding the gray paint sample against the available wood options, she nodded. "Hmm, I guess you're right. It kind of makes for a bad combo."

"Beige it is." he picked up the sample and put it against the wood samples. "Which wood?"

"I like the warmth in this honey oak one. We saw something similar in one of the kitchens and I liked it." She pointed to one particular sample.

"Okay. What about countertops?"

Picking through the samples the builder offered, she found a nice beige one to match the walls. "I've heard good things about this Corian stuff. Solid all the way through and resists scratches and burns."

"We're moving right along here." he added the Corian counter top sample to the pile on the table next to him. "So, do we move to tile or carpet?"

Sam placed the book back on its shelf. Everything was moving along nicely in her life, so why did she feel almost... sad? The house was well under way, the wedding dress design was selected and on it's way, the engagement party was looming closer without her help and Jon had several prospective buyers for his apartment. In all the rush and bother of getting all the plans started for the wedding, they hadn't really talked about their future. Maybe she was scared to bring it up, but what was waiting for her after their marriage?

She loved the bookstore and its two quirky owners, but would she continue to work there after the wedding? It would be a relatively long commute for a wage that they didn't seem to need. And after all, it wasn't like she was running a corporation, it was just a sales job. And the remaining question, what *did* she want to do? Pausing, her hand halfway to the shelf to restock another section of books, it came to her. What she always really wanted to do was go to school. Going back to college was her ultimate dream and maybe now she would be able to do it! She was sure that Jon would support her, as he did in everything else. And if he preferred, she could always go to school part time and find a part-time job to supplement her tuition.

Pleased, and with a lighter heart, she continued stocking the shelves, her mind whirling with the different college courses she had always wanted to take. She was so excited that on her lunch break, she called the local community college and the nearest university and had them send course schedules for the spring to her house. Then she couldn't resist calling Jon at his office.

"'Lo?"

"Hi!"

There was a pause. "Samantha?"

"Yeah. Who else calls you on this line besides your mother and me?"

"You sound funny, I guess. Where are you?"

She frowned. "I'm at work. Can we meet for dinner?"

"I don't know, honey, it looks like it might be a late night." he responded slowly.

Her frown deepened. "Is there anything I can help you with?"

"Not this time. Can I take a raincheck and we'll do it tomorrow evening?"

"Of course." She didn't want to burden him with her own petty thoughts of school while he was in the middle of some important task. "I'll let you get back to work."

"Thanks, sweetie. 'Bye."

As he was hanging up the phone, she heard him talking to someone else in the room. Just before the line went dead, she heard a woman's voice respond. Letting the phone drop back into its cradle, she promised herself she wouldn't panic. It was just his secretary and after all, he was working!

"Sam, is there anything wrong?"

She turned to find one of her bosses, June, standing at the other end of the counter. "Oh, no, of course not." Forcing a smile to her lips, she went back to restocking their new merchandise. Unfortunately, the mindless exercise only left her more time to think and worry.

By the time five o'clock rolled around, Sam was exhausted from avoiding thinking. She picked up dinner on her way home, knowing that the bag full of buffalo wings and french fries was going to be regretted in the morning. Once inside her house, she dropped the bag on the kitchen table and let Molly out the back door. No walk, no park, no frisbee tonight... just greasy buffalo wings and deep-fat-fried french fries.

With a sigh, she settled down at the table with a roll of paper towels, mustard for the french fries and a plate. She was wrist deep in buffalo sauce when the phone rang. Grabbing a paper towel, she wrapped it around the receiver and lifted it to her ear.

"Hello?"

"Sam?"

The quiet voice pierced her heart and she squeezed her eyes shut. "Becki."

"Yeah."

"Are you all right?" Sam's first thought was that there must be something wrong.

"Yeah. I just thought I'd call you while I had a minute. Just... to say hi."

"Oh, well, gee, Beck, that's great! How are you and the kids?" Sam asked, wiping her hands on another paper towel.

"Okay, I guess. The twins are a pain and the little ones are drivin' me crazy, but... that's pretty normal. You?" her voice was growing a little stronger and more confident.

"I'm okay. There's a lot going on that I didn't get to tell you when I was there, but things are okay." Sam returned to the table and sat down. "What's going on with you? Anything new?"

"Nah. Same ol' same ol'. Joe and Rich are never here... I spend most of the day watchin' the kids and cleanin' up after all of them. I sure do miss Mom, even though she weren't much help in the past year. But at least it was a sane adult I could talk with, ya know?" Becki sighed. "I wish you din't live too far away, Sammie."

She cringed at the old nickname. "You could still come here."

"So, tell me all the excitin' things happenin' in yer life."

Not wanting to push her sister away, Sam sighed. "Well, I'm getting married in March."

"Oh. Geez, I guess I figured you and Mr. Moneybags was already married." Becki responded.

"No."

"So where'd you get them nice clothes you was wearin'? And that nice hair-do and makeup and jewelry and all?"

Sam frowned at the envy in her sister's voice. "I worked for them. It's a hard way to live, but I've worked for everything since I left home."

"Was the limo yours, too?"

"That was Jon's idea. He was concerned about driving back to the airport after a trying day." Sam said almost curtly.

"Ya'll call a funeral a tryin' day?" She snorted. "You should walk a day in my shoes!"

"I wasn't given that opportunity."

"Lucky you."

Sam let the silence stretch out.

"I'm sorry, Sammie."

"Yeah, me too. Guess this isn't going to be as easy as we both want it to be, huh?"

"Guess not."

"But Becki, I want to keep trying, okay? I miss you." Tears clogged her throat.

"Yeah, me too. Look, this is gonna cost me money I ain't got. So I'll talk to you again, okay?"

"Next time, I'll call you. And you could write me, you know." Sam gave Becki her address before saying goodbye. Once the call was over, she cleaned up the remaining food and threw it all out. She really wasn't hungry anymore. Her heart felt heavy with sadness for her sister and the closeness they never had. She let an antsy Molly back into the house, then wandered to her bedroom to shower.

Later, curled up on the couch with a book, Sam waited for Jon's nightly call. It was a tradition now, that if they spent the night apart, they at least spoke on the phone before going to bed. While the book was good, she continued to watch the clock, wanting to talk with him about her day's events. By eleven thirty, she found that she was reading one page over and over again. It was at that point she knew it was time to give in. Maybe he was still at work or maybe he went straight home and fell asleep from exhaustion. Either way, it didn't look like they would talk that evening.

Her bed seemed cold and empty, but she climbed in anyway. Molly, sensing her mistress' mood, jumped on the bed and curled up against Sam's side.

"Oh, Mol... could this day get any stranger?" She tried to relax her muscles and invite sleep to come to her, but it didn't. Curling up on her side, Sam pressed her face against Molly's soft fur and let the tears come. Whether it was true sadness, tiredness or fear that brought the tears, Sam didn't know.

Groaning, Jon closed the car door and dragged himself up the sidewalk to Sam's front door. He doubted that she would be awake at one forty-five in the morning, but he just didn't want to go to his apartment. All he needed right now was to lay in her arms and breathe in the sweet smell of her. Work had chewed him up and spit him out today, not letting him rest for one moment until he had given in and gone home.

The house was dark and silent when he closed the door quietly behind him. As his eyes adjusted to the darkness, he heard Molly's toenails tapping along the hallway floor.

"Hey Molly." he greeted her softly, hoping she wouldn't bark and wake Sam up. He frowned as Molly seemed to eye him balefully from the archway to the hall. "What's doin' girl?"

Molly sniffed toward him, scenting him out, but didn't move forward to greet him.

He shrugged and shed his jacket, hanging it on the coat rack in the corner. When he turned back, the hallway was empty. Not giving it any further thought, he strode down the hall to Sam's bedroom. Now that his eyes were used to the lack of light, he could clearly see Sam curled up on the bed. His arms almost ached to hold her, but he stopped to strip off his clothes first. As he approached the bed, he found Molly staring at him from the far side of the room. She was in the corner, watching him carefully, her usual effervescence absent.

"What's the matter with you, girl?" he asked softly. She didn't make any response, just rested her head on her paws and gazed at him. Sliding onto the bed next to Sam, he reached for her warm body. In her sleep, she turned toward him and settled into his arms. Closing his eyes, he pressed against her and drifted off into sleep.

It was only a few minutes later that they were both awakened by an insistent bark and the bouncing of the bed.

Sam's eyes popped open to find Jon's bleary ones blinking at her. "Jon?" She rolled away as Molly barked again and jumped between them. "Molly?"

He pushed himself to a sitting position, gazing uncomprehendingly at the two of them. "What?"

"Jon, what are you doing here?" Sam asked, getting to her feet and glaring at him.

"I left work and came straight here." he said gravelly. "What is *wrong* with her?" They both turned to look at Molly, who was sitting calmly in the middle of the bed.

"What are you talking about? You probably scared the living daylights out of her." Sam told him testily.

"I've been here for almost half an hour. She *saw* me come in, but wouldn't come talk to me. She *watched* me get into bed with you." he informed her. "It's like she was just waiting for me to fall asleep before she pounced on me."

Frowning, Sam looked from Molly to Jon. "Oh come on, Jon, don't be ridiculous. She's just a dog!"

Rubbing a hand over his face, he groaned. "Okay, maybe I'm imagining things. Can we just try to get some sleep. I've got to get back to the office in a few hours."

"Fine." Sam shooed Molly off the bed, then crawled back in and settled under the covers. "Good night."

Not sure exactly what was going on, he lay back down and closed his eyes. He was just nodding off, when the bed bounced again under

Molly's weight. "Not again!" He rolled over to see the mutt pressed up against Samantha's side. "Sam..."

"Just go to sleep, Jon. You've got to get up early, remember?" She didn't even turn over to address him.

"Fine." he rolled onto his side, his back facing the beast and his bride-to-be.

Sam grunted and heard Molly sigh at her side. What exactly *was* Molly protecting her from? It was obvious that she wasn't thrilled about Jon's presence, but why? Jon had spent many a night there over the past few months and Molly had never seemed to even notice. She usually curled up at the end of the bed and slept peacefully. Did the big retriever-mutt pick up on her unhappiness with Jon? Was it that palpable?

By the time Sam tumbled out of the bed the next morning, Jon was long gone. Molly didn't seem to have changed her position at any time during the night. Did last night really happen, or did she dream it all? With a dismissive shrug, she pulled out her clothes for the day. Once dressed, she let Molly out into the yard and went to grab a bagel for breakfast. On the kitchen table was a leftover napkin from the Buffalo Barn, where she'd stopped last night for takeout, with a few words scrawled on it. 'Love you. Call me in a.m. -J' She crumpled up the note and tossed it in the trash. Again, her appetite seemed to leave her, so she let Molly back in the house and left for work without calling. If he didn't have time to speak with her, she didn't have time to speak with him.

It was almost two o'clock before the phone call came for her at the bookstore.

"Samantha?"

"Yes."

"Are you all right? You didn't call me this morning." Jon scolded.

"Oh, I guess I was busy." she pushed a couple of books around on the counter.

"I'm sorry I didn't say good bye this morning, but you were sleeping so peacefully..." he began, not wanting to explain that Molly's brown eyes had almost *dared* him to touch Sam.

"No big deal, Jon."

"Um, okay. So where would you like to go to dinner tonight? I should be able to get out of here at a reasonable time tonight."

"I don't think tonight is good for me." she paused only momentarily. "I have to go." It was petty, but she wasn't ready to let the hurt go, yet. She hung up after his curious goodbye. What was almost as bad, was that he probably didn't even realize what was wrong. After all, he was accustomed to adjusting his schedule for his job and not having to report back to anyone. He probably even thought she understood that last night's call would have to be pre-empted for his work. And he couldn't know about her thoughts of college and the phone call from her sister. Was she being unfair? He *had* come to the house last night to be with her, even if he hadn't woke her. Now she was positive she needed to apologize.

At four-thirty, she told June that she needed to do some errands and would see her in the morning. June waved her off without looking up from her book. Outside, the sun was sitting low in the sky and the air was beginning to cool. A quick walk down the street brought her to the florist shop, where she found a small bouquet of yellow, white and deep purple flowers. It didn't seem too feminine, so she bought it and walked back to her car at the bookstore. Jon's office wasn't too far away, but she hoped he was still there.

At the front receptionist desk, she smiled at the receptionist who recognized her and waved her down the hall. Without looking left or right, Sam strode down the hall to Jon's office. His secretary's desk was empty but his door was closed. Hiding the bouquet behind her back, she knocked softly on the door.

"Come in."

She smiled sympathetically at his tired voice and pushed open the door. Just inside, she froze, her smile going slack. Jon was stretched out on the couch, his tie gone and his shirt open at the neck. His hair was disheveled and his eyes were closed while his blond secretary stood right at his hip. The young woman turned her head and zeroed in on Sam's face.

"Oh! Samantha, hello." she chirped and stepped away from the couch.

Jon's eyes popped open and he focused his eyes on Sam's face. Groaning silently, he knew that this was going to be bad. Not that there was anything going on, but he knew by the look on her face that she wasn't so sure of that. "Sam, honey! What a nice surprise." Slowly, he shifted to a sitting position and smiled at her.

Sam stood in the doorway, unsure of what to do. Miss Patrick's clothes were neatly pressed and her hair perfectly coifed, suggesting that there was no impropriety going on. But still, Sam's heart twisted, wondering what the scene last night would have been.

"C'mon in, sweetheart." he stood and dismissed his secretary with a nod.

The pixie-like woman smiled and slipped out the door, closing it behind her.

"Hello." Sam managed to force out.

He strode to her and went to pull her into a hug. As his arms wrapped around her stiff body, he touched the still clenched flowers behind her back. "Are those for me?"

She brought them out in front of her, staring at them as if she weren't sure where they had come from. "Uh, yeah."

Sighing, he led her to the couch and sat her down. Dropping down next to her, he faced her tiredly. "Okay Samantha, what's going on with you?"

"Nothing."

She was acting strangely and had been since yesterday's phone call. "You're not worried about this, are you?" he swept his hand toward the door and his secretary's desk.

"Of course not." her answer was automatic. She laid the flowers on the coffee table in front of the couch and stood. "I came to see if that dinner invitation was still open, but I see you're busy again."

"Actually, I was just getting ready to leave. I can't take another long night here." He stood with her. "I'd love to have dinner with you."

"I'm not hungry anymore." she murmured, edging her way toward the door.

In the harsh flourescent light she looked pale and tired. There were dark smudges under her eyes and her lips were pressed together tightly. What was with her? She was moody, acting strangely, pale and her eating habits seemed strange and unpredictable. He remembered the napkin on the kitchen table that morning from the Buffalo Barn... did people really eat that greasy stuff? He swayed as a thought hit him hard suddenly. He wanted to sit down, but instead turned to face her fully. "Sam..."

Her tear-filled eyes met his. "What?"

He groaned and went to her, his hand cupping her cheek. "Are you sick? Is there something wrong?" While his gut clenched waiting for her answer, he wasn't sure what he wanted her answer to be.

"I'm fine. Can't I not be hungry? Or do you think that's all I ever think about?" she spat, snapping her head away from his hand. Turning, she reached for the doorknob.

"Wait, honey... please, just wait a minute." he coaxed, grabbing her arm. In his tired state, he couldn't calculate the days in his head fast enough. "Is there something you need to tell me?"

She looked over her shoulder at him, clearly at a loss. "No. I just want to go home."

"Then let me get my jacket and we'll go."

She let him release her and step away before speaking. "I'm going home alone."

The door was open and she was gone before he could stop her. Frowning, he stood still for a moment, wondering if they could have made a baby in the past few weeks. She always took care of the birth control, preferring her diaphragm over condoms, so he didn't really know what to think. But there was no way he could wonder all night.

Sam flopped onto her sofa and squeezed her eyes closed. Molly jumped up on the cushion next to her, her big brown eyes intent on Sam's face. Both sets of eyes found the front door as it flew open and Jon walked in. Molly tumbled to the floor, pressing herself against Sam's legs.

"Jon, what are you doing here?" Sam asked tiredly.

"We need to finish this conversation, Samantha." he started forward, but halted when Molly folded her ears back and growled low in her throat.

They both looked at her in surprise, but she didn't move an inch. Sam placed a hand on Molly's head to soothe her.

"Sam," he lowered his voice, but kept one eye on Molly. "There's something going on and we need to talk about it. You're acting differently and I'm worried about you."

Frowning, she huddled on the couch, her eyes focused on Molly's head. "I don't know what you're talking about." When Jon stepped farther into the room, Molly pressed closer to Sam, the hackles on the back of her head rising slightly.

Eyeing the dog curiously, he wondered if she had some innate sense of Sam's condition or if she was just picking up on Sam's tension with him. "I need to know... Samantha please," he whispered, "are you pregnant?"

She let out a half-laugh, half-sob. "Is that what this is about?" Shaking her head, she clenched her hand on Molly's back. "No, I'm not."

"Are you sure?"

She glared at him and nodded silently.

His shoulders fell, and he eyed her warily. "Then what's going on?" He wasn't ready to explore his feelings on her non-existent 'condition.'

"Look, Jon, if you must know, yesterday was a weird day and you just weren't available for me. I used to be able to handle everything on my own, I didn't need anyone. Since you've come into my life, I've become dependent on you and your responses to me and that's wrong." she leaned her head back on the couch and stared at the ceiling. "I need to get back to the place where it's me I depend on... I rarely disappoint."

He had to strain to hear her last words, but no matter how softly they were spoken, they still hurt. "Samantha, I didn't know..."

Rolling her head back and forth, her voice was almost toneless. "No, you didn't. You were busy at work and I can't blame you for that. You have responsibilities there, and they're important to you. I thought a lot about this and I understand that sometimes work is foremost for you. I just have to learn to listen to myself more and not rely so much on you."

"That's not what I want! You must know you come first to me." He eased his way into the living room and sat in the chair. "I'm so sorry I had to work late last night."

A tear rolled silently down her cheek and she wiped it away with a fist. "If you'd only stopped to call me... just two minutes to hear your voice... I guess I'm selfish but I wanted to know that you didn't forget me. Nine-thirty went by, and then ten... by ten thirty, I knew you weren't going to call. But I waited..."

"And I didn't call." he said softly, thinking of at least a dozen times when he'd wanted to hear her voice. But he thought if he just pushed himself a little longer, he would be able to go home to her. And each minute ran into an hour... "I'm sorry, honey."

"And when I was ready to apologize, to throw myself at your feet for being petty on the phone with you..." she paused again, seeing them in his office. "I knew you'd be tired and I was ready to be at your beck-and-call... and there you were, with that woman hovering over you."

"You know there's nothing between Miss Patrick and me." he stated clearly.

She sniffled. "In my head, I know that. But my heart saw the two of you in there, and I couldn't help feeling betrayed. Like you were spending your time with her and not me." She held out a hand tiredly before he could speak. "It's business, I know. But no one ever said the heart was a logical thing."

He wanted to go to her side, but Molly was still glaring at him. "Tell me what happened yesterday."

"I called you, wanting to share my ideas about going back to school after we're married..." her voice trailed off. "I thought you would be proud of me. But you were busy so I decided it would wait until our evening call. After talking to you, I just felt put-off, so I stopped and got dinner... and of course eating that stuff made me feel worse. And in the middle of dinner, Becki called."

"Is she all right?" his voice was filled with concern.

"Yeah. She wanted to talk. I tried to convince her to come here, she ignored me. I told her we were getting married and about taking care of myself these past years. We argued, of course..." her lip trembled. "I wanted to tell you about it. When things happen to me now, my first thought is always of you. Of sharing things with you, or asking your opinion. But I didn't call you, didn't feel I could interrupt. But we'd never gone a night without being together or talking on the phone, so I figured we'd update each other..."

"And I didn't call." he repeated.

"No." she whispered. "You didn't. And I sunk lower, wondering what could be so much more important than us. I told you, Jon, I'm not used to this."

"I'm so sorry. I guess you're right, I'm used to being trapped at work. Things have been fairly light until now, but work always picks up toward the end of the year. Budget work, internal audits, end of the year calculations, all that stuff. I like to have my hand in it, to know what's going on under my nose. I guess I forgot that I'm part of a we, now. I'm not accustomed to that, either." He inched his way toward her by moving to the far end of the couch. Molly watched him with eagle eyes.

"Everything feels so unstable right now. I feel like I'm in the middle of a really long transition and I'm not sure when it's going to end. We haven't even talked about plans for after we're married... what am I going to do? How are you going to commute to work every day? What's going to change in our relationship? What do you expect of me and what do I expect of you? What about a family? We've never even talked about these things... Is it too late? What if we find we don't agree on things?"

"Samantha, whatever we don't agree on, we'll work out. We love each other and I know we'll be able to deal with anything that comes up. As for after the marriage, we can talk about that anytime you like. All you had to do was say something... if you're worried, you need to speak up about it so we can address it." He gave her a teasing smile. "You don't seem to have a problem speaking up about this engagement party... that's just a few hours. What we're talking about is the rest of our lives... don't be shy about that."

She reached out a hand toward him. "Jon, I'm scared."

The beast be damned. He slid across the couch and pulled her into his arms. "Don't be scared, sweetie. We have each other. We can depend on each other, even if we each have to be reminded of that every now and then."

Chapter Fifteen

Spring catalogs and class schedules arrived at Sam's house the next week, making her giddy with excitement. She hadn't pushed the conversation with Jon, but knew she wanted his opinion before making any other move. But what harm could a few catalogs do? There were so many classes she wanted to take and so much she wanted to learn. She had the catalogs spread open on the kitchen table when Jon arrived.

"Hi, honey." he kissed the top of her head then dropped into the chair across from her. "Whatcha lookin' at?"

"Catalogs for the local colleges. I was thinking of going back after we got married." she said tentatively.

He reached out and spun one of the books around to face him. "Oh?"

"Yeah, well, classes actually start the end of January, so maybe Spring won't be such a great idea. But it'll give me a head start on decisions for next fall." she responded, turning a few pages in her catalog.

He had the schedule of classes in front of him, indicating the spring semester's beginning and ending dates. If she took classes starting in February, she'd still be in school for their March wedding and they would have to put off the honeymoon. If she waited until the fall to start classes, there would be less stress on her, but what about children? "What kind of degree were you thinking about, sweetie?"

Brightening at his interest, she smiled and said, "I think I'd like to teach, maybe English?"

Looking up at her, his heart melted. She was like a kid, all bright-eyed and sparkly. "Yeah? You need a four-year degree for that?"

"Yes. But I could start out at the community college, then transfer to the university, if that's what we decide. Community college is cheaper, of course."

He smiled. "Don't worry about the money. If the university is where you need to go, and you can get in, then that's where you'll go."

"Oh, Jon! This is all I've ever wanted! A loving, supportive husband and an education for my future. And I think I'd love to teach the underprivileged, to let them know there's a way out if they work hard enough." she clasped her hands together and leaned forward. "I feel like there's so much I want to learn! College was always my big dream."

"If it's what you want, then you should go for it." He wanted to scream and beat his fists on the table. There was no way she would want to go to school and raise a family at the same time. Fulfilling his father's second stipulation was racing farther and farther out of range. Could he encourage her to get pregnant and then hire a nanny while she was in school? Gazing across the table at her, he knew that he was being selfish. How could he take this dream from her? "Maybe you should go talk with a counselor and see what you need to do to prepare for entry in the fall."

"What a great idea!" Her smile was broad as she thumbed through the catalog looking for the University's phone number. "Maybe there's some studying I can do over the summer to get back up to speed for the fall."

When she looked away, his shoulders sagged. What was he going to do now? He wanted Samantha to have every opportunity to fulfill her dreams, but what about his business? Why didn't he think about this before? Looking back at her, he sighed inwardly. It wouldn't have made any difference. She was the woman he loved and nothing could change that. He would give up his whole company to be with her, without ever looking back.

"You know, I could even take night classes or weekend classes at the university. They have all these alternative class schedules so maybe I could work while going to school." she suggested.

He met her eyes, shining with such love and excitement that he couldn't help but smile. "Why don't you try a semester full-time and see what it feels like. Then you can decide what other things you might want to do." She would really only need to be pregnant by the spring after their wedding... shaking his head, he cleared the thoughts away. The decision was made. He was going to have to forfeit full ownership of the company, remain 49% owner and deal with a board of directors and stockholders.

"My mother would be so happy to see me in school again. I loved it during the two semesters at the community college. I can't wait." she hugged the catalog to her chest, interesting classes already highlighted.

"Just sit here for a minute." Jon pushed her into the chair at his dining room table. "And close your eyes."

Sam heaved a big sigh and squeezed her eyes shut.

"No peeking!" he called out.

"I'm not!"

He carried in a small ice cream cake with a Snoopy dog decorated on it. There was a circle of candles around the cartoon dog, lit and blazing. "Happy birthday!"

Her eyes popped open and she grinned at the small fire in front of her. "Oh, how cute!"

"I promise not to sing!" he pressed a hand to his heart and grinned. "I've lost many a relationship that way. Quick, make a wish and blow out the candles before my sprinklers go off!"

Smacking his arm, she leaned over and blew out the candles in one puff. "Where did you find this cute design? I love Snoopy!"

"I found a good picture and had the ice cream place copy it." he sliced a piece of cake off and slid it onto a plate. "It's chocolate ice cream and chocolate cake."

She dug in and tasted the sweet confection. "Yummy!"

"I just knew you'd like it." he grinned and took a forkful from his own plate. "So, did May and June give you a gift?"

"May gave me a lovely crystal bud vase and June gave me a book of poetry." she answered in between bites.

"I'm guessing May is the more creative of the twins."

Grinning, she shrugged. "June knows I like poetry. I guess she figured it was an easy buy."

"Well," he finished his cake. "How about my gifts?"

Her eyes lit up. "You bought me something?"

"A trinket or two." Standing, he pulled her from the chair and into the living room. "Sit."

She did, then held out her hands in front of her, palms up.

He dragged a big black trashbag from behind the couch. "Now, for the fun stuff. But mind you, I don't wrap gifts."

"Jon, you're spoiling me!"

"Good." He opened the bag and stuck his arm in. After fishing around, he pulled out a black Trapper notebook.

"Oh!" she clapped her hands together and began bouncing up and down on the couch. "For school!"

He nodded and handed her the notebook. "It's one of those things that closes with velcro so you won't lose anything."

"As if I ever lose anything!" she said sarcastically and rolled her eyes. "At least I've never lost a bill!"

"Not yet. Just the party list, the option lists for the new house, the ad for my apartment..."

She stopped him by pressing a kiss to his lips. "Thank you, darling. Now I'll never lose any of my school work. Will you be pinning my mittens to my jacket?"

Grinning, he reached into the bag again and moved some things around. "Guess I won't give you those mittens I bought."

"Oh shut up!"

"Hey, be happy I didn't go and buy you pens and pencils and an eraser." he straightened, but didn't withdraw from the trashbag.

"Thank goodness!"

"Sike!" he pulled out a carton of pens, pencils and erasers, along with a package of lined notebook paper.

She giggled and pushed him away. "You're such a dork!" But she took the items and inspected each of them, then added them to the notebook.

"But wait, there's more!" Out came a voice-activated mini-tape recorder and a package of tapes. "So you don't miss anything important during those long, boring... um, I mean, *informative* lectures."

She squealed and inspected both items with delight. "This is so cool! I just can't wait to get started!"

"Just a second there, missy. That ain't all."

"Jon!"

He pulled his last item from the garbage bag and held it out. "Every student needs a book bag."

Laughing, she grabbed the black and tan backpack out of his hands. "Look at all these cool pockets!"

"And the back is padded so you don't get hurt when you have a lot of heavy books to carry." he explained.

"This is so cool, Jon!" she began packing her gifts away into her new backpack. "I'm going to be more prepared for college than I ever was in my entire school career. I don't think you've forgotten anything."

"Whoops, wrong again, honey." He lifted a small briefcase-like bag and set it on her lap. "Go on, open it. Every good student needs one of these nowadays."

With trembling hands, she unzipped the soft-sided case and lifted the top. "No way!"

Grinning, he watched her touch the plastic casing. "Way."

"This is just... amazing! A laptop computer?" she turned shining eyes on him. "I've never owned any kind of computer."

"Top of the line, just for you."

She smoothed her hand over its top, then flipped it open. "I'm floored. And I have absolutely no idea how to use it!"

He laughed and touched the power button for her. "Don't worry, I'll teach you everything I know."

"Oh look!" she pointed to the screen. "I've seen this before."

"Probably at my office. It's the current rage in operating systems." He touched a few buttons and a box with information popped up. Point, he read off the computer's specifications to her and assured her that it was all top of the line.

She groaned and leaned back against the couch. "Of course, I should have known that!" Rolling her eyes, she slid him a look. "I have no clue what you just said. It sounded a little like Latin."

"Don't worry, you'll understand everything when I'm through with you." he rubbed his hands together. "Lets start with what's important... how to turn it on and off."

"Okay, Mister Smarty-pants." she smacked at his hands. "You just wait. In a couple of months, I'll be running circles around you."

"I don't doubt it." he murmured, watching her press keys and play with the touchpad.

"Maybe I'll be running your company for you by the end of next year."

He winced at her innocent comment, thinking she was closer to the truth than she knew.

The engagement party was the 17th of November, just one week after Sam's 28th birthday. After much discussion, Sam did purchase a new outfit, but a casual one from one of her regular discount stores.

When they were dressed and ready to leave her house, Jon stopped Samantha in the foyer. "You look great."

She picked at a piece of lint on her navy blue sweater, then tugged the hem down over her waist and the matching ankle length full skirt. "It's kind of plain. I'm sure your mother is going to look superb." The ivory-colored blouse peeking out from under the sweater was a tasteful vee-neck with matching tiny embroidered flowers bordering the vee.

He shrugged off her comment. "My mother has her own style... as do you. You're always classy-looking, lady. Don't feel like you need to compete with my mother. You're both beautiful in your own ways."

"Thank you." She turned to go.

"Wait, I have something for you." he held out a jewelry box.

"Another gift? You already gave me my birthday gifts." she protested.

"This is an 'I love you' gift."

She flipped open the box and gasped. On the dark blue velvet lay a pin of beautiful pastel blue, pink, yellow and lavender flowers with pastel green stems and leaves. The bouquet was tied together with a pretty gold bow at their base. "Oh, Jon! How beautiful!"

"Let me help you put it on." he plucked the pin from the box and stepped forward. "I saw it and knew it would bring just the right colors to your blue outfit."

When he finished, she hurried to the hall bathroom to see it. He was right, it was the perfect accent to her dark blue sweater and ivory blouse. Returning to his side, she gave him a long, lingering kiss. "Thank you. Again."

"Sheesh, I feel kinda like a bum next to such a beautiful lady." he said sheepishly.

She snorted as she looked him over. He was wearing dark khaki pants, a matching oxford shirt and a brown sports jacket. "You've got to be kidding. You look very masculine. *Muy macho.*" she teased with an accent.

"Quit that." Taking her hand, he led her out to the car. "We'd better get going or we're going to be late for our own engagement party."

She frowned and worried all the way to the house. But as soon as Jon opened the front door, there was a smile on her face.

"Samantha! Jonathan!"

They turned in unison to find Alaria hurrying to greet them.

"Mom, I hope we aren't late." he hugged her.

Alaria released him and turned to Samantha. "Of course not. You're right on time. Samantha, darling." She hugged the younger woman. "You look lovely. And what an enchanting pin!" Leaning closer, she inspected it.

"It was a gift from Jon."

Nodding, Alaria slipped an arm around Sam's waist and drew her toward the family room. "He has good taste. Especially in women." She winked at Sam and hugged her closer.

Sam blushed and looked over her shoulder to find Jon already engaged in conversation. "He's a wonderful and giving man."

"Like his father was." Alaria agreed.

"You should have seen all the gifts he gave me for my birthday last weekend." she was glad for the comfortable topic.

"Do tell." Alaria found two glasses of punch and handed one to Sam.

She took a sip before explaining. "I'm going back to college come summer and he bought me all my supplies." Giggling, she didn't notice Alaria's look of surprise. "You know, notebook, pens, pencils, paper, backpack, tape recorder and the like."

Alaria's expression was clear yet interested when Sam looked up. "How sweet."

"And to really show his support for my education, he also bought me a laptop. I can't wait to learn all about it so I can use it for my schoolwork." she continued.

"Jonathan knows how important education is to one's self-esteem. Because it's always about how you see yourself, not how others see you." Alaria said sincerely.

Sam looked at Alaria with renewed respect. "Now I'm positive that Jon got his values from you."

Alaria smiled and grasped Sam's hand in hers. "Thank you, my dear." Straightening, she tugged Sam along with her. "We might as well start making the rounds now. Don't worry, you won't have to remember everyone's name."

Alaria finally left Sam engrossed in a literature conversation and went to find her son. She pulled him from a loud debate on stocks, edging him toward the den.

"Mom, what's going on? Where's Samantha?" he demanded.

"She's fine. Stop worrying about her." Alaria closed the doors behind them.

"Then what's this about?" he gestured at the empty room.

"Your Samantha was boasting to me about your lavish birthday gifts." she began.

"Oh c'mon. The laptop was the only expensive part and I got a good deal." he defended himself.

"Sweetheart, it has nothing to do with the gifts themselves. It's the reason behind the gifts." She paused to let him explain. When he remained silent, she frowned. "She said she's going back to school this summer."

"That's what she wants to do."

"But what about the will?" she whispered.

"That's really my business, isn't it? I have every right to follow through, or not, as I see fit, yes?"

"But Jonathan..."

He held up a hand to stop her. "I want Samantha to be happy. She wants to finish college, so that's what I want."

Alaria studied him for a moment. "The company..."

"Will survive." he interrupted again. "I'll still have partial control and will be able to have input as to its future. You and Dad wanted me to understand that love and family are important. Well, I've found out they aren't just important, they come first no matter what. Business is business, Mom, but Samantha is my whole life."

She smoothed a hand over his hair, thinking he looked so much like Frank when she met him. If only Frank had learned his lessons that early. "I support your decisions no matter what, Jonathan." she said softly.

He turned away and reached for the doorknob.

"Jonathan?"

Looking over his shoulder, he waited silently.

"I'm so proud of you."

He gave her a small smile, then left her alone. Once out in the hallway, he released a breath. He hoped the hard part was now over.

Sam looked up as Jon slipped an arm around her waist and hugged her close.

"Excuse us." he apologized to the two women across from them, then guided Sam away. "Have you eaten?"

"Not yet. You?"

"Nope. Let's go see what Mom had cooked up for us." Leading her over to the buffet table in the dining room, he inspected the table.

"Oh look, fancy little sandwiches and crackers with cheese and grapes." She leaned into his side and tried to stifle her giggles.

"C'mon now, I'm sure everything tastes great." he paused. "Do you think we'd have to eat everything on the table to get filled up?"

She picked up a white china plate, a fork and a napkin. "Something here must be edible." Several finger sandwiches went onto her plate, along with a fistful of crackers and several slices of cheese. She broke off a little stalk of grapes and added it to the food already on her plate. "Gee, where's the caviar?"

He followed behind her, setting food on his own plate. "Don't say that too loud. She might whisk in and add it to the spread already here."

"Oh, here's some potato and pasta salads on the sideboard. Ooo, and a chicken caesar salad... now we're talking." She made room on her plate and added scoops of the different salads.

"Salads, blech. What's the point?" he frowned and looked around. "I keep expecting to find a plate of turkey or roast beef hidden behind a plant for me."

"You'll just have to make do with what we have here." She nudged him as they headed for the patio to sit down. "So, what were you and your mom talking about?"

He looked over at her in surprise. "What?"

"I saw the two of you secret away to the den." she said as he pulled a chair out from a lawn table for her.

They set their plates on the table. "She was just making sure everything was all right." he lied.

She frowned and popped a cube of cheese into her mouth. "Uh huh. And?"

"And what?"

"Is everything all right?" She chewed on a grape, then scooped up some potato salad.

"Of course it is." Taking a bite out of the tiny sandwich, he looked up at the darkened sky. "It's a beautiful night for a party. Not too cold, yet."

"Smooth change of subject, sweetheart." she teased.

He shrugged and ate another finger sandwich. "Just making a comment."

"Was your mother upset about something? Did I do anything wrong?"

His eyes flew to her face, realizing that she had no clue of his guilty feelings. She was merely concerned with making a faux pas and embarrassing his mother. "No, Samantha. She wasn't upset with something and you didn't do anything wrong. She was just being my mother."

She looked up at him through her eyelashes. "You promise you'll tell me if she's unhappy with me for some reason?"

Leaning over, he kissed her cheek. "I promise. But it won't happen."

They ate in silence for a few minutes, then were joined by Alaria.

"How is the food?" she asked.

Sam smiled. "It's all very good. I love the caesar salad."

"Good! I know that Jonathan isn't too fond of salads, but this caterer specializes in 'lite fare'. And since he practically demanded that the evening stay casual, I thought this food would be perfect." Alaria replied.

He rolled his eyes. "The least you could have done was sneak in a *real* sandwich for me!"

Alaria turned to look at her only child. "Who says I didn't?"

A grin spread over his face and he bounded up from the table, heading straight for the kitchen.

"He's a good boy, but stubborn sometimes." Alaria looked at Samantha. "I hope you're having a good time."

"Oh, I am. All of your guests are very nice and I'm enjoying the food." Sam picked up another grape and rolled it between her fingers for a moment. "I just want to thank you for everything you're doing. I'm not accustomed to having people do such nice things for me."

Alaria gazed at the young woman sitting across from her, wondering what else she had missed out on. "I'm more than happy to do it. All of it! But don't worry, I'll try not to meddle too much." she teased as Jonathan returned.

"Mmm! You're my favorite mother." he said, kissing her cheek before sitting down. He had brought with him another plate filled with a huge club sandwich, potato chips, pickles and a beer. "Now *this* is a party."

Alaria sighed and stood. "You're hopeless, Jonathan."

He grinned and took a big bite out of the sandwich. "And you love me." he said around the food.

"Oh." she shook her head and walked away.

He turned to Sam and smiled, chewing happily.

Chapter Sixteen

Thanksgiving and Christmas went by in a blur for Samantha. Both were celebrated at Alaria's home and both included a great amount of delicious food and intimate evenings. They were the first major holidays without Frank Edwards, so both evenings were quiet and reflective.

Once New Year's had passed, uneventfully as Sam worked the "Midnight Madness" celebration at the shopping center where the bookstore was located, time seemed to speed up. Sam started getting more and more nervous about the wedding. All of the sudden, it was just over eight weeks away! The house was due to be ready in February, just after Valentine's day, and then the wedding was scheduled for March 6th.

Just a week into the new year, it was Sam's turn to call Becki.

"Y'ello?"

Sam froze, wondering how she had managed to call Becki every other weekend and never speak to Joe. Her luck was bound to have run out at some point. "Is Becki there?"

"Yah, but she's busy. Who's this?"

How was she supposed to answer that? "It's Sam."

"Sam, who?"

She didn't think he was smart enough to try and make her uncomfortable, he just didn't know who she was. "Her sister."

"Oh, so it's you, is it? What in the hell do you want?" he demanded.

"I want to speak with Becki. Put her on the phone, please." she said stiffly.

"I won't. She don't need you meddlin' in her life. She's perfectly happy now that you gone back to where you belong." his voice was loud and angry. "And yer pretty Becki reminds me of yer momma in *so many ways*, that I don't even miss her none."

Sam gasped and gripped the phone tightly. "You go get Becki right now!"

He cackled into the phone and then hung up.

She placed the receiver back in its cradle and stared blindly out the kitchen window. He was just torturing her... Becki would never...

The phone rang right next to her and she swivelled to pick it up. "Hello?" Her shoulders sagged in relief when she heard the operator ask if she would accept a collect call from Becki. "Of course, yes."

"Sam?"

"Becki! All you all right?" She sounded far away.

"Yeah, I'm fine. You just called at a bad time, is all." Becki responded.

"Is he still there?"

"Nah, he stormed out right after he hung up."

Sam hesitated, then blurted out, "Is he forcing you to sleep with him, Beck?" There was a static-filled silence for a moment.

"Only if he comes home really drunk." she answered softly.

Holding in a sob, Sam closed her eyes. "Please, Becki, come out here. Get away from him! You'll never be whole there."

"Sam, I wouldn't know how to get by without someone takin' care of me. And I got the kids to support, ya know." she sighed. "Your way is just a dream to me."

"Jon and I will help you. You won't be alone and you won't be under anyone else's thumb anymore. Can you imagine being responsible only to yourself and your kids? Being free to see friends and go out for a walk in the evening." Sam tried to convince her. "Look, at least come out for the wedding. You can come out early and spend some time with me and just *get away*."

"Temporarily, right?"

Sam crossed her fingers. "Of course! Just come visit, see the bookstore, the house, spend some time with Jon. There's plenty of room for you *and* the kids."

"Let me see what I can figure out, okay? No promises."

"You just tell me the date and I'll send out plane tickets. You guys will have a great time visiting here." Sam only hoped that once she got Becki and the kids out of that man's house, they would never go back.

February 1 was the date of no return. Becki and her kids were due to fly in at three o'clock and Sam spent the entire morning arranging and rearranging the temporary accommodations at her house. Sam and

Becki were going to share the master bedroom with the queen sized bed, which was plenty large enough for the two of them. The baby and the second youngest would share the spare room, where Sam had setup a cot that Alaria lent her along with the daybed already installed there. The twins and the middle child would sleep in borrowed sleeping bags in the cleared out dining room. It was going to be tight, but Sam wanted her family with *her*. Alaria offered, time and again, to put up the entire family in her big, empty house, but Sam refused. She wasn't aware of how well-behaved, or not, Becki's children were going to be and she didn't want to put Alaria through anything uncomfortable.

"Samantha, relax." Jon called from the kitchen, where he was reading the paper. "Becki doesn't care what your house looks like or where they're going to sleep. She's just going to be happy to be with you."

Sam stood in the kitchen doorway, wringing her hands together. "I'm doing the right thing, right?"

He turned. "Sweetheart, you aren't going to tie her to a chair... you're just going to make it very attractive to stay."

She slid onto his lap and hugged him hard. "Thank you for helping me with all of this. You're so good to me, sometimes it's scary."

Nuzzling her neck, he asked, "Why?"

She closed her eyes and leaned her head back. "Because things that seem too good to be true, usually are."

"Did I forget to tell you I snore?"

Laughing, she pressed her forehead against his. "I found that out the hard way."

"Hmm, what about the toilet seat problem?"

"That could be a deal-breaker, I must admit."

He kissed her. "I'll remember that." Looking at his watch, he gave her one last kiss on the shoulder, then pushed her to her feet. "We should get going."

"All right. Let me get my purse."

"It was nice of May and June to let you cut back your hours so drastically until after the wedding." he called after her.

She reappeared and they headed out the door. "Yeah, they're being very sweet about the whole thing. But January was the inventory month, and it's usually pretty quiet until the spring. Not too many book-giving holidays for a few months."

Outside, they climbed into the mini-van Sam had rented the day before and set off for the airport. Since Becki and the kids were going to be in town for over a month, it seemed reasonable to rent another larger vehicle to get around in, instead of always driving squished into two separate cars.

"I hope their flight was okay." she worried, wishing she was driving so that she had something to concentrate on. "And that the kids don't get sick. They've never been on a plane before."

"You didn't get sick the first time you flew." he reminded her.

"But they're just kids."

He looked over at her clenched hands. "It's going to be okay, Samantha. They're going to be fine."

"What if the kids are unhappy here?" Looking out the window, she wondered if they would see her hometown as big and cold compared to where they lived.

"How could they be unhappy?" he asked, negotiating the traffic near the airport. "They'll have an aunt who dotes on them and spoils them rotten. They'll have a neat house with a big yard and a dog to play with! Only blocks away is a great park where they'll be sure to find some kids to play with, even in the cold."

"The house is so small." she said in a timid voice. "We'll probably kill each other after the first week."

"Mom's offer still stands. She'd be more than happy to have a full house! And she'd dote on those kids worse than you would." he reminded her.

"I can't. I just don't know Becki's children well enough. I don't want to threaten my relationship with her over the kids."

"Mom doesn't scare so easily. But it's still your decision." He finally found a parking space near the doors. "Lets go. If the plane is on time, then they should be landing soon."

It was almost deserted inside the building, even though flights were scheduled to arrive and depart. Three o'clock on a weekday just wasn't prime travel-time.

"Gate three, honey." Jon called to her once he found the flight listed on an overhead board. "And it looks like they're only running five minutes late."

Sam nodded and took his hand, walking with him toward the arrival gate. There was no plane in sight, but she couldn't sit still. Jon on the other hand, she saw, had no problems dropping into a chair and picking up a stray newspaper. She paced, stopping frequently to stare hard out the window, as if willing the plane to appear. Finally, it did, and she waited anxiously while the plane 'parked' and the hallway connected to it's door. People began straggling out and all of the sudden, she panicked. What if they changed their mind and weren't on the plane? What if they missed it and were calling her at home right now? What if...? And then, there they were, walking quietly out of the hall and into the open room. Quickly, Sam looked her sister over, noting her weight loss and drawn face. Then she sprung into action.

"Becki!" she called out, waving and walking toward the brood. "I'm so glad you all made it!"

Becki turn and smiled tiredly. She herded the kids toward Sam, carrying the youngest in her arms. "Yup, we made it. Barely."

"Well let's find your bags and get you home so you can all rest from your big adventure!" Sam said brightly. "We'll introduce everyone around once we get in the car, okay?"

Becki shrugged and moved the kids toward the baggage area. "We were lucky the plane was almost empty. The kids were kinda noisy."

Looking at the quiet group of children, Sam couldn't imagine them being rowdy. "What do your bags look like?"

They collected a luggage cart and Jonathan helped the twins stack the family's bags on it. When they had everything, the group marched outside to the minivan. The bags were transferred silently from the cart to the van, then both boys returned the cart to an attendant. Loading the kids into the van was done just as quietly, and then they were on the road.

Sam turned around in her seat and spoke brightly. "So, let's all get to know each other." She smiled, then continued. "I'm Sam, and this is Jon." she pointed to him.

"I'm Thomas and that's Christopher." One of the twins announced from the back.

Squinting, Sam saw that Christopher had a sulky look on his face and his hair was shorter than his twin's. "Hi Thomas and Christopher. I remember when you two were born." Both had shades of Joe in their faces.

"I'm Brian." said the child, trapped between the twins.

"How old are you, Brian?" Jonathan asked.

"I'm nine."

Sam wished she could take notes. "And what's your name, sweetheart?" she asked the little blond girl sitting next to Becki.

"Sarah." she answered shyly.

"And is that your little sister?" Sam pointed to the toddler on Becki's lap.

Sarah nodded.

"What's her name?"

"Mary." Sarah practically whispered to Sam.

Mary, tired of the whole conversation, stuck her thumb in her mouth and closed her eyes.

"Well, I'm sure glad to know all of you." Sam told them.

"What do we call you?" Brian piped up from the back.

"Well, you can call me Sam or Aunt Sam. Whatever makes you comfortable." she answered. "I've got a room for the two girls and then you three boys get to camp out in the dining room with sleeping bags." She saw Christopher's mouth tighten, but he continued to stare silently out the tinted window. "But if you guys aren't careful, my dog might just sneak into your bag while you're sleeping."

"You got a dog?" Thomas asked curiously.

"Yup."

"Is it a big 'tack dog?" Brian wanted to know.

Sam laughed at the thought of Molly being an attack dog. "No way. She's too silly to be an attack dog."

"What'ser name?" Thomas again.

"Molly. She's a big golden-haired mutt." She looked down when Sarah tugged on her sleeve. "Yes?"

"Is she scary?"

"Nah. She just likes to jump around and lick people." Sam answered.

"Sarah is afraid of dogs." Becki jumped in, speaking for the first time since they got in the van.

"I'll protect you, Sarah." Jon met her eyes in the rear view mirror. "Don't worry, Molly won't hurt you."

Sarah remained wide-eyed, but said no more.

"Are you sure you have enough room for us all, Sammie?" Becki asked, shifting Mary in her lap to a more comfortable position.

"Of course. We might be a little cramped, but nothing that a good romp in the park won't cure." Sam smiled before turning back to face the front of the car. "It'll be like a big sleep over."

Unloading the van was a simple affair. Sam grabbed two bags and headed for the front door, while Jon swung Sarah into his arms before following.

"Now don't you worry one bit, Sarah. Molly just loves to play with pretty little girls. And she's got soft fur and floppy ears to play with." he reassured her as he entered the house.

Molly was busy dancing around Sam for the moment. "Hiya, sweetie." she greeted the happy canine. "Look, I brought you some playmates."

Molly, as if understanding, whipped around and began wriggling joyfully at the people spilling through the front door. She wagged her way from one person to the next, sniffing and licking hands wherever she could. Seeing a creature tucked in Jon's arms, she danced around and nudged a dangling shoe.

Jon laughed as Sarah tried to climb over his head. "It's okay, Sarah. She's just trying to say hello. Why don't you give me your hand?" When she did, he held it out, barely within Molly's reach.

Molly sniffed the fingers, licked her, then turned to follow one of the boys into the living room.

"See? She just wants to know who you are." he explained.

Sarah clutched at his shoulders, her eyes following Molly's every move.

"C'mon Sarah, let's go see your room, 'kay?" Sam suggested.

Jon followed her down the hallway, Sarah still clinging to him. "Look, you get to share a room with Mary so you won't be lonely. Is that okay?"

She nodded and let him put her down on the floor.

Becki appeared in the doorway. "The boys are out back with the dog already."

Sam turned to look out the window. "I hope they're okay here, Beck."

"They're fine. I think Christopher misses Joe and Richard. He liked to trail after them, sometimes." Becki answered, looking around. "You girls should be okay in here. And Momma will be right next door, see?" She led them out into the hallway to show them where Sam's bedroom was.

Looking across the room at Jon, Sam let her shoulders sag. "I hope they're okay here." she repeated quietly.

He pulled her into a hug. "It's going to be okay, honey." They walked out into the hallway, then found Becki and the girls in the living room. "Bet you guys are gonna be hungry soon."

Becki looked at the old watch looped around her wrist. "Not me, but them boys can *always* eat."

"How about we order in some pizza?" he suggested. "We can just hang out, eat greasy pizza, and relax."

"Sounds okay to me." Sam agreed.

Becki shrugged and nodded. "Sure, pizza'll do."

Sam stared up at the ceiling in the darkness, her ears perked to every noise. So many children in the house made her hyper-sensitive to all the groans and sighs of the house itself. Turning her head sideways, she made out her sister's form on the mattress next to her. "Becki?" she whispered.

"Yeah?"

"Did I wake you?"

"No."

Sam saw Becki shift on the bed. "What was it like after I left?"

Becki sighed. "Actually, it wasn't much different then when you was there. Joe made Momma miserable all the time, Richard was the little prince, and I was the family whore."

"How could they treat you like that after..." she fell silent.

"Joe claimed that if I hadn't been runnin' around with all them boys, he wouldn't have gone after me. He said he was just another John who got more than he bargained for." Becki's voice was flat. "The boys really didn't make no difference, Sammie. Nothin' made no difference. Joe was Joe and he never changed."

"What about Richard? Did he come after you, too?" she shuddered.

"Joe was pretty hard with Richard, sayin' we was related by blood so I was off-limits."

"Did Joe continue to force you to sleep with him after the twins were born?" Sam asked quietly.

"Joe never stopped forcing me, 'specially if he was drunk. Once the boys was born, Momma tried to keep an eye on him, and took a lot of his anger to keep him away from me. But once Momma got sick, that was it, he was all over me again." Becki covered her eyes with her arm. "And once she passed, it was like I slipped right into her place."

"How is it that you didn't get pregnant by him again?" Sam wanted to know.

"Oh, he was careful after the twins was born. Said he didn't want none of my diseases from the other boys."

"I wish I had known."

"What was you gonna do, Sammie? You had to take care of yourself. Momma and I wanted you to get out."

Sam sat up and wrapped her arms around her own waist. "It wasn't right for you two to make that decision without me."

"I already knew the hell of Joe. We weren't gonna let him suck you in, too."

"And now, Becki? What about now? Do you want to go on being his whipping girl?" Sam kept her eyes trained on a spot on the wall. "Now I *can* help you. And I don't want you to go back."

"What'm I gonna do? I got no place to go, no skills to take care of my family. At least with Joe, I know we're gonna get fed and we got a roof over our heads."

"You just have to think in a whole new way, Beck. You guys can stay here for a while, until you get a job, then we can help you find a bigger place. Getting you a job shouldn't be too hard... we can find you something in retail, like I do. It's not going to be easy, but it's something I know you can do." Sam tried to convince her.

"I'm not strong enough, Sammie."

Putting a hand on her sister's arm, Sam said, "If you're strong enough to stay with him, then you're more than strong enough to leave."

"I don't know..."

"Please, then just think about it while you're here. Keep an open mind?"

"I'll try."

"No matter what you decide, I'll always be here for you." Sam paused. "And I'm really glad you're here, Becki."

"So come with me."

Becki shook her head and set her coffee cup down on the kitchen table. "What about the kids?"

"Well, you said yourself that the Christopher and Thomas can take care of Brian here, and we can bring the girls with us. I want you to see the dress." Sam prodded.

"I said the boys're okay when they're home alone at *our* house." Becki corrected.

"Well, it's not so different here. They can't break anything and the neighborhood is a good one. No one will bother them."

Becki frowned and played with her cup. "Well, I guess it's all right. As long as we're not gone too long."

"Good!" Sam jumped up. "Let's get our stuff together. We need to leave soon so I can make my appointment."

Becki got up slowly and followed her sister from the kitchen. The three boys were outside playing in the back yard with the dog. Going to the back door, she opened it and called out to them. When they looked up, she spoke. "Aunt Sammie and I are goin' out for a little while. We're takin' the girls. The three of you behave, okay?"

They yelled back a chorus of okays before going back to wrestling with Molly and each other.

Shutting the back door, she went to the girls' bedroom and gathered them up. "We're goin' for a ride with Aunt Sammie."

Sarah lept up from the floor, her pig-tails flopping behind her. "Yay!"

Mary just held out her arms to be picked up.

"Ready?" Sam asked from the doorway.

"Yea, sure."

They trooped out of the house and into the minivan.

"Madame Vue is a real character. And she's so fussy about how the dress looks. I hope there's not too much altering to be done... so we won't be too long." Sam babbled as she drove toward the boutique.

Becki just nodded and watched out the window. When they pulled into a parking space, she looked around. "Are we here already?"

"Yup. The shop is right there." Sam pointed to the boutique in front of them.

"I thought it was farther away." Getting out, Becki helped Sarah from the van, then took Mary in her arms. "You sure it's okay to have the girls with us?"

"Sure!" Sam took Sarah's hand and the foursome walked into the boutique. Madame Vue spotted them right away, and her round face lit up.

"Samantha! You are here! And you bring guests!" Madame called out.

Sam grinned and hugged Madame. "Yes, I brought my sister Becki, and my nieces Mary and Sarah, to see the dress."

"Non, they are here to see *you* in the dress!" Madame turned and engulfed Becki and Mary in a hug. "You are beautiful, oui! I find dresses for all of you for the wedding, oui?"

"Oh, what a wonderful idea!" Sam clapped her hands together.

"No!" Becki exclaimed. "We... couldn't."

Leading the foursome into the back room, Madame ignored Becki's protest. "We have something lovely for all of you in Madame's shop."

Becki tugged on Sam's shirt. "Sammie, we can't afford new dresses."

"It will be my gift to you, Beck. I wanted you all to be here, and I want to spoil you all. We'll have to bring the boys to get suits at Jon's tailor." Sam waved away her sister's worries. "You wait and see, you'll love it."

In the back room, Becki sat on the couch with Mary in her lap. Sarah trailed Madame Vue wherever she went, but managed to stay out from under her feet.

"Samantha, you go and get yourself undressed so we can get you in the dress, oui?" Madame instructed.

Sam disappeared behind a curtain as she was told.

"You." Madame pointed to Becki. "You are very small, petite..."

Becki nodded silently, Mary huddled against her.

"And you have color like your sister, oui? We must have you in something pastel and light..." Madame clucked as she hurried off to get Samantha's dress. "I will find for you!" she called back to Becki.

"Auntie Sammie?" Sarah called, peeking her head around the curtain to see her aunt disrobing. "Could I throw flowers at you?"

Sam blinked and stared at the small child, who seemed to have blossomed overnight. "Of course you can! What a wonderful idea... you and Mary can be the flower girls. We weren't going to have any, because we didn't have any younger relatives in the area. But now that *you're* here, the wedding will be perfect!"

Sarah whipped around and grinned at her mother. "We get to be flower girls!"

Madame whirled back into the room, Samantha's dress on her arm. "Here, here is dress. You wait for my help." Then she trotted back out of the room. When she came back, the was carrying a long lavender and ice green dress. "For you. Go try on." Madame then slipped behind the curtain and began helping Sam get into her dress.

Becki stared at the dress hanging next to a curtained dressing area. It was too pretty and dainty for her. One hitch of her pointy elbow, and she was sure the delicate fabric would rip.

"Mama, I'll take care of Mary. Go try on the pretty dress." Sarah helped Mary down from Becki's lap, then the two girls sat quietly on the floor, Mary cuddled in her big sister's lap.

Standing, Becki crossed the room and took the dress behind the curtain with her.

Madame Vue helped Sam pull the wedding dress on, then began buttoning the tiny pearl buttons up the back of the dress. They were stitched into the lacy fabric so that they barely showed at all. "Bah, this doesn't line up so right." she murmured, pulling a notepad from her pocket. "We fix it." Once marked down, she then circled around in front of Sam, inspecting the bodice and neckline.

"Madame, this is lovely." Sam touched the beautiful lace fabric on her sleeve. "I can't believe it's for me."

"Of course it is for you!" she clucked. "Come out into the room so we can look at the train... then I will get the veil." When Samantha walked out into the room, Madame spread out the train behind her.

Sam grinned when Mary and Sarah clapped delightedly at her. "Auntie Sammie, you're bee-yoo-tee-ful!"

"Thank you, sweetie!" she blew a kiss at Sarah.

"Stand here." Madame directed her to the mirror, then spread the train out behind her. "It is long enough?"

Sam looked behind her, gasping at the beautiful lace designs on the satin train. It was at least five feet long! "Oh, it's long enough!"

"Good. Stand still! I get the veil." Madame disappeared again.

"Auntie Sammie, you look like a princess." Sarah said wistfully. "I hope I look like that someday."

"I know you will, honey." Sam answered, tentatively touching different parts of the dress, almost afraid it would disintegrate under her fingers.

Madame returned with a frothy white veil attached to a circle of white flowers. She carefully placed it on the back of Sam's head, then pinned it in place. The veil trailed down Sam's back to just below her waist. "I think it is good, oui." Across the room, she picked up a polaroid camera, then started taking pictures of Sam. "Just in case the eye misses it, the camera will find it."

When the picture-taking was over, the veil came off and Sam ducked behind the curtain with Madame Vue to take the dress off.

"Mama, are you still there?" Sarah called out shrilly.

Becki was still standing in the curtained dressing room, her eyes riveted on the mirror in front of her. *Is that really me?* "Yes, Sarah, I'm still here."

"You comin' out?"

The dress was just a bit too wide around the waist, but the rest of it flowed over her angles, softening them into curves. After five children, she never would have believed she still *had* curves. "In a minute, baby." When she finally emerged from behind the curtain, Madame Vue had already stored away Sam's dress and was waiting for her.

"Oui! Perfect for your coloring! We can get matching colors for the babies..." Madame circled Becki, pinching and tucking at different places. "Let me take some measurements, and I will fix."

Sam finished dressing and then joined her nieces on the floor. "Doesn't Mommy look pretty?"

Sarah was transfixed on her mother. "Yeah. Like a ballerina. She needs flowers in her hair."

Becki's cheeks turned pink as Madame fluttered around her.

"You look so pretty and smiley. I want to look just like *you* when I grow up, Mama." Sarah whispered.

Becki looked at her daughter, her eyes shining with love. "I just want you to be happy, always, Sarrie... and Mary, too."

Sam caught her sister's eye and smiled. "It's not so bad being happy, Beck. You should let yourself try it once or twice."

Chapter Seventeen

The final walkthrough on the new house was scheduled for the tenth of February, at eleven in the morning. Sam left Becki with the minivan and instructions on how to get to the nearest shopping center, then she and Jon headed for the new house.

"Oh Jon, I'm so excited! I can't wait to see the house."

Jon rolled his eyes and grinned as he drove. "You just saw the house a month ago, Samantha. Not too much could have changed at this stage of the game."

"It's different. This final walkthrough is it... then we go right to the lawyer's office for settlement." she bounced up and down on the car seat. "We're going to have a *home*."

"Yeah, well, it also means we're in debt up to our ears." he grumbled.

She shook her head and looked out the window. "I'm not going to let you bum me out. Next to our wedding day, this is going to be the best day of *our* life."

"Look, let me just prepare you for this walkthrough. We're going to go over that house with a fine-tooth comb. Anything that looks wrong, we point it out. Anything in question, we bring it up. Understand?" he said.

"Yes, master." she stuck her tongue out at him. "I can be critical, trust me."

"Because this punch list becomes binding with the settlement this afternoon." he continued.

"I understand that." Pausing, she thought her words out carefully. "Has the apartment sold yet?"

He frowned. "No, we had that one bite, but they couldn't get the financing. I'm sure someone will buy it, though. Why?"

"Well, I haven't put my house on the market, yet."

"I just figured we would sell it after we're all moved into the new place. That way you didn't have to worry about people tromping through the house while you're still living there." He slowed down to take the exit.

"Oh."

"What, 'oh'?" he asked, glancing over at her confused look.

"I guess I'm having trouble understanding how we can afford the new house without having sold either of our current places. I mean, I know I can sell my place without any trouble. Houses in my little neighborhood are hot right now." she told him.

"I have some money put away that we're using for the down payment. And besides, what if you want to keep your place? Like say, for Becki?" He turned into their new development, slowing the car to the speed limit.

"I guess I figured the house was too small for Becki's family." she said quietly, thinking that Becki's family could stay in the new house with them, using the spare bedrooms and finished basement.

"I know it's small, sweetie, but it means independence for her. And you know how crucial that is. She won't want to be a burden. And moving out of Joe's house and into her own would be a real self-esteem lifter." Turning onto their street, he changed the subject. "Thar she is."

Sam's gaze flickered from Jon, to their new house set back from the street. "Yeah, thar she is." Forgetting their previous discussion, she grabbed his arm tightly and exhaled loudly. "I can't wait to live here!"

He watched her animated features, loving the happiness he was sharing with her. "Not too long, now... Soon you'll be Mrs. Samantha Edwards."

"And we'll live happily-ever-after here... together."

"C'mon, they're waiting for us." he pointed to the group assembled on the front porch. "Let's get a move on, my darling wife-to-be."

Jonathan flopped into the wing chair facing Simon's desk. "Well, the punch list was long, but most of it was minor. The few major repairs they have to make can be done by their estimate of February 15th."

"Great." Simon leaned back in his chair. "Where's your lovely bride-to-be?"

Rolling his eyes, Jon tilted his head. "Bathroom."

"Ah." Simon nodded and pushed some papers around on the desk. "The builder's representative should be here within the half hour. Then we can get this all finished and you two can make your next step." Looking over Jonathan's shoulder, Simon handed him a packet of neatly folded papers. "You need to look these over and get them back to me before your birthday."

Jonathan frowned. "What are they?"

Waving his hand, Simon harumphed them away. "Legal stuff about the will. You'll need to sign it and get your mother's signature as well."

"Couldn't this wait for another time?" Jonathan glared at the older man, aware that Samantha could walk in at any moment.

"Don't forget this marriage needs your mother's stamp of approval." Simon explained.

That earned him another glare. "I'll take care of your damn paperwork." Jonathan stuffed the packet in his jacket pocket. "And then that will be the end of it."

"You must have forgotten, dear boy..." Simon was interrupted by Samantha's appearance in the doorway.

"Hello Simon." she greeted the lawyer. They had met previously at one of Alaria's parties. "How are you?"

The paunchy man stood and shook her hand. "I'm well, thank you, my dear. Please, sit, sit! Would you like some coffee?"

Jonathan snorted. "You didn't offer *me* any coffee."

"*You* aren't a beautiful young lady." Simon smiled at Samantha graciously.

"No, thank you, I'm fine. Is there anything we need to go over before the others arrive?" She looked from one man to another, wondering at the tension in the large room.

"No, no... everything is ready and waiting in the conference room. Nothing to fear, we're all set." Simon assured her.

"Good! I'm so excited you can't imagine!" she grasped Jon's hand and gave it a squeeze. "I thought I would never be as excited as the first time I bought my house... but this is so much better!"

"Yeah, because now you get to share the burden." Jonathan teased.

"It looks like our party has arrived." Simon spotted the two men walking down the hall. "Shall we meet them?"

Jonathan stood, letting Simon greet the other lawyers. When Samantha brushed by him, he felt her hip graze the papers in his pocket. His eyes shot up to meet hers, guilt tugging at his conscience, but she was smiling happily at him and reaching for his hand.

"Let's go get our house." she whispered, pressing a kiss to his cheek.

He smiled stiffly and let her pull him out of Simon's stuffy office to join the others in the conference room down the hall.

They were lucky and got a bite on Jonathan's apartment only two days later. It was a young woman who was moving into town to start a new job. Her job was due to start at the end of February, so Jonathan didn't have to be moved out until then. Even so, when the fifteenth came, and the builder agreed that they were finished with the major work, Jon and Sam were both ready to begin moving things into the house. They discussed his options and decided Jon would go ahead and move in before the wedding and get a feel for his commute and even possibly set up a home office where he could work a couple of days a week.

Samantha stood in the library of the new house, looking over the furniture that had just arrived for Jon's office/library. It was big, dark, warm polished oak furniture that was the exact opposite of his modern-looking office downtown. There was the big executive desk with an ell for the computer, the matching towering bookshelves and office automation table. They had ordered three phone lines for the house; one for all purpose, one for the fax machine and one for a modem connection. They had yet to purchase a desktop computer for the house, but already had the fax machine, copier and telephone setup in the room. Across from the desk was a comfortable tan sofa with blue and brown pillows on it, where one of them could keep the other company in the room.

Jonathan walked in the room carrying two file boxes. "Wow, it looks nice in here!"

"Yup. You sure have good taste in furniture, mister."

Setting the boxes on the floor next to the new executive chair, he grinned. "I knows what I likes," he approached her. "And I sure likes you."

She let him pull her into a hug. "Good thing, since you're stuck with me."

"Damn straight." He turned to go back to the car to bring in more boxes.

"Want me to unpack some of those file boxes for you?" she offered.

"Nah, don't worry about that boring stuff. Let's get the stuff for the kitchen so we can see what we have duplicates of. Maybe you can give some of the leftovers to your sister?" he suggested as they walked back out to the minivan in the driveway.

"Good idea. I just hope she wants to stay."

"Well, if she decides to, then we'll do what we can. If she doesn't, then we have to accept that it's her life and her decision. Right?" he asked pointedly.

"That doesn't mean I'm going to give up for good." Following him back into the house with a box full of silverware and plates. "It just means I have to be persistent."

He grunted as he set his two boxes on the floor in the breakfast nook. "I don't know. If you push too hard, you may push her away."

"Jon, he's still abusing her."

Straightening, he frowned angrily. "I surmised as much. But we can't make the change for her. All we can do is give her a safe secure place to be."

She crossed her arms over her chest and sighed. "It makes me sick to my stomach to think about it. And to think about all those years..."

He stroked her hair away from her face. "It's not your fault. If you were there, he probably would have abused you as well."

She shook her head silently, knowing that Joe would never have touched her. In his eyes, she was a pig, and not good enough for any man.

"We'll do the best we can, honey, to convince her to stay." Tugging her back toward the front door, he changed the subject. "You know, they're delivering the rest of my furniture this afternoon..."

"Yeah?"

"The dining room, the living room..." he paused dramatically. "The bedroom."

She giggled as he wiggled his eyebrows comically at him. "Oh no you don't! We talked about this."

Groaning, he followed her back to the minivan to retrieve more boxes. "So we did. But I believe I was under some kind of medication when we came to that decision."

"Hey, it was either we not make love in the new house until after we're married, or we not make love at *all* until after the wedding." she reminded him.

"I liked option C. You know, the one where we make love in every spot conceivable during every available moment." he called after her.

The furniture arrived on time and they directed Jon's living room set into their new living room, having decided that his furniture was a bit more formal than hers. The dining room set went into the new dining room, since it went nicely with the living room furniture in the adjacent room. They sent the bedroom furniture up into the master bedroom, Jon assisting with the navigation while he grinned lewdly at Sam. When the movers were finished, they locked up the house and went back to Sam's for dinner with Becki and the kids.

"Sam." Becki's voice was urgent and worried when they arrived.

Sam took one look at her sister and hauled her away to the master bedroom. Once the door was shut tightly, she whispered, "What happened?"

Becki's hands were shaking as she wrung them together tightly. "Joe called."

"What did he want?"

"He wants us to come home. Now." she whispered back, fear lacing her voice. "We have to go."

"No, Becki, you don't. You came here for the wedding and it's still over two weeks away." Sam explained patiently.

"You don't understand. If we don't go back now, there'll be hell to pay when we do get back." Tears shone in her eyes. "It's just easier to go now."

"Then don't *go* back. He has no right to say what you can and can't do. You aren't married to him, and you're way past legal age. You can do what you want, when you want and where you want!" Sam said hotly.

"But the boys are his kids. He has a right to demand they come home."

Sam pushed her sister to sit on the bed. "Becki, what does it say on their birth certificate where it asks for 'father'?"

Becki paused and looked down at the bedspread. "Unknown. Because they didn't believe me!"

"Then he has no right to those boys. They're yours and yours alone unless he chooses to try and prove otherwise. You're their mother and you say what happens and what doesn't happen when it comes to them and to you."

"He'll come after us, Sammie. He'll come out and get us and then I'll really get it." Becki cried. "I don't want to go through that."

"We'll stop him. We'll get a court order to keep him away..."

Becki stood, shaking her head and babbling tearfully, "No, we have to go. We have to go right away."

Sam stood with her. "Okay, look, there aren't any planes out tonight. Just wait overnight and I'll take you to the airport tomorrow morning. If you still want to go."

"I'll call him and tell him. We'll go home first thing tomorrow morning."

Watching Becki pick up the bedside phone, Sam cringed and turned away. If they went home, she was sure they would never come back. Leaving her sister to make her call, Sam rejoined Jon and the kids in the living room.

"Problem?" Jon asked as she stood at the fringe of the room.

She met his wary gaze with bleary eyes. "He called. They're going home tomorrow."

"What?"

"I tried to talk her out of it, but she won't listen." Suddenly, Sam realized the kids had stopped playing and were looking at her. With a snap, she shut her mouth.

"Auntie Sammie? We're leaving?" Sarah squeaked.

"I'm sorry sweetie, I should have let your Mama tell you." Sam said sadly to the little girl.

"But I don't want to go!" Sarah hopped up and crawled into Jon's lap. "I like it here. I want to stay here with you."

"Well I don't." Christopher said bluntly. "I hate it here. And I'm glad we're leaving."

Becki joined them, her shoulders low and her eyes bleak. "It doesn't matter what any of you want or don't want. We're goin' home tomorrow."

"What about the wedding?" Sarah asked. "Me and Mary won't get to be flower girls?"

"Maybe you'll be able to come back just for the wedding." Sam suggested. "Your Mama and I will talk about it."

Sarah began to cry and buried her head in Jon's chest. "I want to stay!"

Jon stood, hugging her to his chest. "You'll come back and see us again, sweetie." he promised, carrying her back to her room.

Becki watched them go, then turned back to her other children. "Pack up your things. We're leavin' first thing in the morning."

Christopher immediately began putting his clothes into his suitcase.

"Mama, I want to stay here, too." Thomas whispered, standing right at her side. "I don't want to go back to him."

Sam almost cried out at the look on his face. No little boy should be frightened of going home.

"We're leavin' first thing in the morning." Becki repeated before leaving the room.

Jon reappeared at Sam's side. "I left her with Becki."

Sam turned away from the kids and went into the kitchen, knowing Jon would follow. Turning, she pinched her nose. "How can I let them go back?"

"You don't have a choice, Sam. You have to let them go."

She closed her eyes. "I want to help her so much."

"She's not ready to be helped. Just keep at her, honey, and one day she'll come to you, knowing you'll be there." he assured her. "She won't leave until she's ready."

"But will that be too late?" she whispered.

Sam walked back into her house after seeing her sister and the kids off at the airport. She could still feel Sarah and Thomas clinging to her sides. Jon had parted ways with her outside the house, needing to go directly to work. Only Molly was home to greet her, and even the big dog seemed dejected at the emptiness of the house.

"I think it's time for some spring cleaning. Lets go through that spare bedroom and get it all packed up for our move. I'm sure there are things we can throw away, too." Sam told Molly. "Keep ourselves busy, that's the key. Maybe then we won't miss them so much." Armed with several boxes and trashbags, they walked down the hall together. In the spare bedroom, the smell of little girls hit her. Sinking to the floor, she let the tears fall.

Molly whined and curled up next to her, resting her head on Sam's thigh.

"C'mon now, we can't let it get to us. Think of what we have to look forward to! My goodness, so much happiness to come!" Getting to her knees, Sam opened a dresser drawer and began emptying it into a box. "You'll have a big new house to explore, a new yard to run around and a new park to play in! And me! Whew, I'll have a husband! And a new house to take care of, and school to go to! And we'll keep in touch. I'll write to the kids, and talk to Becki every weekend."

It took her the better part of the day to pack up the spare room. By the time she was done, the room looked as if no one had lived there for years. The boxes were stacked neatly in the front hall, labeled and ready to be moved. Exhausted from all the exertion, Sam plopped down on the sofa and closed her eyes. Jonathan was due shortly, and they would share dinner and conversation. It was going to be a pleasant, quiet evening alone with her fiancé... she should be thrilled to have the time alone with him. So why did she feel so sad?

It had been so much fun spending time with her sister and the kids. Even when Christopher had remained sullen, the rest of them had warmed to her easily. Sarah was so cheerful and bright, eager to learn and do whatever was asked of her. Thomas was so responsible and mature, wanting only to be a proper little man. And although Brian was quiet, he was smart and responded easily to his brothers' teasing. Little Mary wanted to be just like her older sister, following Sarah around day and night. They were the family she'd craved as a child, and was now being deprived of again as an adult. It seemed that no matter where she went, Joe haunted her. He was manipulative with her mother while Sam was growing up, and just as dominating with Becki now.

No man had the right to manipulate the rest of the world to suit himself. She would persist, continuing to convince Becki to leave that place. Even if it took years, she would not give up. She had not known enough to save her sister so many years ago, but there was no such excuse now. These people that she now held so dear, would not slip away again.

"Becki, are you sure you won't come back for the wedding? I can still get plane tickets for you and the kids." Sam prodded. "I want you all to be here!"

"Sammie, he just won't hear of it." Becki answered.

"Just overnight! We'll show him the non-refundable tickets. It isn't right that he's keeping you from your only sister's wedding."

"I'm sorry, Sammie."

Closing her eyes, Sam clutched the receiver tightly. "You don't have to tell him. You could just leave while he's at work."

"He'd kill me when we came back!"

Sam took a deep breath. "You don't have to go back." Silence met her whispered statement. "All right, I'm sorry. But I can't believe that you won't be here. This is supposed to be the happiest day of my life and I want you to share it with me!"

"I wish I could."

"Maybe I could talk to him." Sam offered, the thought making her cringe.

Becki's bark of laughter cut right through the phone lines. "I don't think that'll work."

"Me, either." She sighed, her heart squeezing painfully. "Well, I guess that's it. I'll talk to you again next Saturday. And I'll ask one last time then."

"And I'll have to say no again, Sammie. I wish you would let this drop."

"I want you here so badly, I can't let it drop." Rubbing her eyes, she said goodbye and hung up. The wedding was just two weeks from today, with still no hope of having her sister and the kids present.

The days since their departure seemed quiet and empty. She tried to keep busy, packing and preparing for the wedding. And the next two weeks were going to be tight, what with last minute meetings with Alaria about the arrangements. Caterers, florists, musicians all wanted final meetings to confirm plans. Alaria had offered to take care of it, but Sam wantcd to kccp as busy as possible.

Meanwhile, Jon's apartment was empty and he was officially living in the new house. During the evenings, when they weren't both exhausted, they were moving boxes from Sam's house to the new place. The next call to Becki seemed to roll around too quickly.

"Don't even say it, Sammie." she warned. "I hate to say no again."

"Then don't!"

"I'm sorry."

"In one week, I will no longer be a Velmar. I'll be a married woman, starting a new life. I want you and the kids to be a part of that life." Sam insisted.

"And we will! But from a distance." Becki responded.

"Can't you just ask him one more time?"

"Sammie, if I ask him again, it'll just make things worse 'round here."

Sam cringed at her sister's blunt words. It hadn't occurred to her that Joe was punishing Becki for just asking about the wedding. "I'm sorry, Beck. I just wasn't thinking."

"People who don't live this life, just don't understand."

"No one should ever have to understand, especially your children." Sam whispered.

Becki half-laughed, half-sobbed. "I know. But I can't change it."

"When you're ready, you know I'll be here, waiting for you."

"I hope you don't get tired of waitin'."

"Never." Sam promised tearfully. "Not for you, and not for your children."

"That's the last of it, sweetness." Jonathan kissed Sam's cheek as they surveyed her empty house. "Just the last of the furniture in your bedroom and whatever clothes are left."

"I can't believe this is the last day I'll be single."

"That's right, tomorrow you get fitted for the old ball and chain." he teased.

"If you only knew!" she grinned. "First I get primped and coifed, then stuffed into a dress and rolled down the aisle."

"Ha! More likely you'll float down the aisle. I mean, after all, you *are* marrying me!"

She smacked his arm. "Okay, mister smarty-pants, get on outta here."

"All right. I'm off to Mom's house. I'll see you tomorrow at one o'clock. Don't be late." he gave her a lingering kiss, then departed.

The schedule for tomorrow was going to be grueling, but she doubted that anyone was going to let her get away with being late. The appointment at Adolfo's was for ten a.m. and the limo was due to pick her up at noon. She was expected at the church at twelve thirty for final touches with Madame Vue in the bridal chambers.

After much argument, mostly with Alaria, they had decided against a rehearsal dinner. It wasn't really a necessity since there was no formal wedding party. Sam and Jon would be standing up alone, throwing tradition away. She was even going to walk down the aisle alone, which fit her feelings of giving herself to Jon, instead of someone else giving her away.

But for the moment, all Sam wanted was some peace and quiet. Tomorrow was going to be the best day of her life, even if Becki and the kids couldn't make it. She knew they would be there in spirit, sharing her joy long-distance.

Settling down on her bed, with Molly next to her, Sam closed her eyes. Her whole life was about to change! The man she loved, and who loved her just as desperately, was going to be her mate for life. They would build a future together, learning and loving, making a family! And she was going to do everything to make her husband happy. There was nothing she wouldn't do for him, all he had to do was ask.

As her mind wandered, she realized that there was one more stop to add to her schedule tomorrow. She wanted to leave Molly at the new house so she wouldn't be wandering around this empty place all alone. It was bound to be a long day, and she deserved to be with the things that reminded her of home... and right now all those things were in the new house.

"C'mon, Molly, lets go." Sam opened the car door and Molly jumped out onto the driveway. "Here's your new home! Remember it? You were here last weekend with us."

Molly raced around, sniffing the newly planted trees and bushes, marking them as her own.

"Inside, Molly." Sam called, shooing the roving mutt through the front door.

Obediently, Molly trotted through the front door and right into the library.

Sam followed, not wanting her to wreck any of Jon's work items. Fortunately, Molly was just meandering around, sniffing at corners and under the desk. Shaking her head, Sam eyed the stacks of papers piled on every inch of desktop space. As she brushed past a precarious stack, it fell over onto the floor. "Oh, darn!" Bending down, she scooped up the stack and looked around. There was not a spare square of space on the desk, and she didn't want to mix up his papers. With her free arm, she pushed the chair back away from the desk, thinking she would set the papers on his chair for him to rearrange later. Rolling her eyes, she spotted some papers already on the chair. Maybe she could figure out where this stack went if she just glanced through it. Thumbing through the top pages, she saw what looked like some legal papers with both Jon's and her name on it. When Alaria's name jumped out at her, she became curious.

She read the top page once, then twice. Her hands shaking, she skimmed through the remaining papers stapled to the first page. Her stomach clenched and she doubled over, feeling as if she were sucker-punched. *It's not true!* she screamed silently. The floor seemed to roll away from her and she grasped for the corner of the desk to steady herself. *Not true, not true, not true.* she chanted to herself.

She dropped the sheaf of papers haphazardly onto the desk and stumbled from the room. Her blood pounded through her veins as she automatically set out food and water for Molly, then returned to her car. It took her two tries to start it, and she drove blindly back toward town. He wouldn't, he couldn't... but it was all there in print, signed and sealed. Maybe if his scrawled signature hadn't been at the bottom of the paper, she could have held onto the doubts. But it had been there, dark and thick as blood.

Adolfo welcomed her with fervor, not noticing her strange behavior, only that she was ten minutes late. Sam didn't bother to pay attention, letting them push her to and fro, readying her for the big moment. For the biggest lie of her life.

"It's time, dear."

Samantha turned toward the church's assistant with a blank face, flowers clutched tightly in her hands. "Yes, all right." How could she be going through with this? Yet she walked out of the bride's chambers, lips pressed closed. The music swelled out from the doorway across from her, where everyone was waiting for her appearance. She placed one foot in front of the other, forcing herself forward, blocking all thought from her mind.

Jonathan fidgeted, his eyes locked on the entrance to the room. The music went on and on... and then there she was. She filled his vision, everything and everyone else fading away as she glided down the aisle. He didn't see her tight features or her stiff form, only saw the woman he loved more than life itself, approaching him. She was so beautiful that it almost hurt his eyes.

Expectant faces turned toward Sam as she stepped into the doorway. The church was decorated with beautiful white flower arrangements placed strategically throughout the room. While each arrangement had been approved by both Alaria and Sam, now they looked ostentatious. Sam's head reeled and her nostrils flared as the aroma of fresh flowers assaulted her. White satin bows hung gaily from the end of each pew, taunting her at every step.

Alaria smiled up at Sam, sniffled quietly and dabbed a tissue to her eyes.

Jon watched as his bride-to-be floated toward him, her head high, her eyes sparkling. He could only pray that this was turning out to be the wedding of her dreams. Just a few more steps and she would be there, with him, forever forward.

When she finally reached his side, Sam placed her hand in the crook of his arm, as she had been instructed in practice. He was smiling down at her, so tall and proud in his tuxedo. Without realizing it, a tear slipped down her cheek... but then all conscious thoughts were forced from her mind as the ceremony began. She didn't want to think, didn't want to do anything but get this over with. She was suddenly glad that

Becki wasn't there to witness her downfall. The best day of her life was turning out to be the worst.

Chapter Eighteen

Sam didn't remember the ceremony ending, didn't remember getting into the limo for the ride to the reception and didn't want to remember the shining, smiling faces that greeted their announced entrance. The party was a mere blur, faces melding in and out of each other. She thought that Jon did a lot of talking, but she couldn't be sure. What she knew was that he hadn't let go of her once since she took his arm in the church. When she looked at him, she saw him smiling and laughing and she supposed that she was doing the same. She couldn't be sure.

Once out on the dance floor, he pulled her close. "Are you all right, sweetie?"

She nodded mutely and stared at his shoulder.

"You must be exhausted! Just a little longer and then we can disappear." he promised.

Was that good or bad? She wasn't sure she wanted to be alone with him. What would she say?

It was several hours before they could actually leave, but when they did, Sam wasn't any closer to knowing what to do next. She let Jon help her into the limo, but scooted to the far side of the bench seat, resting her head on the smooth leather headrest.

Jon closed the limo door behind him, then told the driver to take them home. "Home." he said out loud, looking down on his new bride. "Doesn't that sound wonderful?"

She closed her eyes and kept her lips pressed tightly together.

"What a long day for you, sweetheart. Did you eat anything at all? I saw you picking at the food on your plate, but didn't actually see you eat any of it." he took her hand and squeezed it.

Sighing and rolling her head back and forth, she let her hand lay slack in his. The drive back to the house was taking forever. The space in the limo seemed to be getting smaller by the minute and she was afraid she was going to suffocate.

"Don't worry, honey. When we get home, we have time to rest before our flight out Monday morning. We can just veg out and be together." He scooted closer and pressed a kiss to her flushed temple.

When the car rolled to a stop, Sam gathered up her skirts and practically jumped out, hurrying to the front door. Darn! It was locked. She would have to wait for him after all. When Jon finally joined her, she stepped aside to let him unlock and open the door. As he turned back to her, she brushed past him into the foyer, then disappeared.

"Samantha!" Confused, he followed after her, finding her in the library. "You didn't let me carry you over the threshold."

She stood in the middle of the room, eyes trained on the floor. Without thinking, she pulled her head-piece and veil from her hair, then threw it onto the couch. "I thought this would be the appropriate place to speak with you."

Frowning, he watched her warily. "What are you talking about?"

She turned toward his desk and flung her arm out over the mess of papers. "This is what it was all for, wasn't it?" The rage that had simmered in her stomach all day was bubbling up. All of the sudden, she was that terrified sixteen year-old again, facing the step-father who had nothing but insults and degrading remarks for her. "How could you do this to me?"

He set his hands on his hips and stared at her. "Do what?"

Stepping forward, she leaned over and swept several stacks of papers from the desk out into the air where they fluttered to the floor. "How could I have been so blind?" She began picking through the pile in the middle of the desk, her hands shaking so badly she dropped several pieces of paper. When she finally found what she was looking for, she turned and advanced on him. The papers clutched in her hand were thrust out in front of her body like a sword. "THIS! This is what you *did* to me."

His heart sinking, he took the papers from her. Had he left the will on his desk? Unfolding the packet, he realized it was the stack that Simon had given him when they signed the settlement papers on the house. "Sam..."

Her hands clenched at her sides, she glared at him. "Don't! There's no way to explain this! I read it, I saw your signature, I know what it all means." Laughing harshly, she closed her eyes. "That's right, you need a woman, just go out and find the pitiful fat chick who has no one, romance her and she'll fall right into your trap."

"*Samantha.*" his voice was full of anguish as he crumpled the papers in his fist.

"If you had just told me up front, then at least we would have *both* known exactly why we were going into this marriage. No misunderstandings, no complications, *no hurt feelings.*" She felt like she was going to throw up.

"I love you." he growled through clenched teeth.

She dropped her head back and nearly howled. "No more lying!"

"This," he shook the papers in front of her. "Is nothing! It has nothing to do with you!"

"It has everything to do with me, *Jonathan.*"

He cringed and dropped his hand to his side.

"You wanted to save your company, and marrying me was the only way to do it. You used me... you've *been* using me and lying to me since you met me!" She blinked and Joe's face floated in front of her, sneering and reminding her that no man could ever love her. "Well here you are, you have your beloved company. What else did I miss? Do I have to bear you a son? Give you the heir to your throne?"

He sucked in a breath. "I didn't force you into this, Samantha. You agreed wholeheartedly to marry me."

"When I thought you really loved me! If I had known..."

"But you did." he interrupted. "You obviously found this *before* the wedding. Why did you go through with it? Why not humiliate me by leaving me at the altar? Why not have the satisfaction of seeing me lose my company, something obviously so precious to me that I would do anything to keep it?"

She raised her chin and stared him right in the eyes. "Because I would *never* hurt someone I love that way..." *The way you hurt me.* Without another word, she stomped past him and up the stairs.

His shoulders slumped and he stared at the floor. Even after learning of his deceit, she could still admit to loving him. If only he could make her see how much he cared for her.

Upstairs, Samantha bypassed the master suite and went into the big empty 'in-law' suite. Closing the door, she crossed the room to the windows. It was all a farce, a big elaborate scheme to keep from losing his company. Scratching at the door made her turn. When she opened it, big brown eyes looked up at her from a furry face. "Molly." Letting the dog into the room, she closed and locked the door, then sank to the floor, her dress smushed up around her. Molly sat next to her, leaning her warm, heavy body against Sam's side. "What am I going to do, Mol? What do I do?"

Jon stood in front of the closed door for almost ten minutes, before finally knocking. "Samantha?" Silence greeted his query. "Samantha, please open the door so we can talk about this." He thought that two hours cooling off time was long enough and now they needed to deal with the situation.

"There's nothing to talk about." she called through the door.

"Yes, there is. You haven't given me an opportunity to explain. Don't I at least deserve that?" he asked.

"No."

He sighed and leaned his forehead against the door. "I love you, Samantha. My father's will only made me realize that I didn't want to be alone forever. You coming into my life was my fate being sealed."

Sam sat silently on the floor near the door. She didn't want to hear his story because she knew he would talk his way out of this. No matter what he had done, she still loved him. But she wasn't sure if she would ever be able to forgive him or trust him. What kind of relationship did that leave them with?

"Samantha, I'm sorry I didn't tell you about the will. I didn't think you would want to be with me, and I wanted to be with you very much."

"You lied to me, Jonathan. You used me to get what *you* wanted. You would have married anyone to keep your company. Well, I hope you're happy, because it's all you're going to have." she finished in a whisper.

"The company isn't mine, Samantha. I'll get to keep less than half of it, the rest will become public stock. I wasn't willing to do what it takes to make the company 100% mine. What I did, conveniently, was try to keep a part of the company in the family. Will or no will, I would have married you because I love you from the depths of my soul." he pleaded with her.

"I'm glad that I was convenient. But didn't you know, Jonathan, that flowers and sweet words would have won over almost any woman.

You didn't need to scrape the bottom of the barrel." She ignored his pleas of love, knowing that if he loved her, he wouldn't have hurt her this way.

"Stop that! Stop putting yourself down. I wanted you and I did what I had to in order to get you. Do you want me to give away the company? I'll do it if you want me to! If it will make you come back to me, I'll get rid of it all together. Whatever it is you want me to do, I'll do it, no questions asked." he promised.

"I want you to tell me that you didn't really do this."

"I can't do that." There were tears in his eyes as he forced the words out of his mouth.

"Then I can't stay." She opened the door suddenly, and stepped away as he staggered forward, thrown off-balance. "I've never let anyone hurt me since the day I walked out of my mother's house. Until today."

He sucked in a breath, seeing her tear-streaked face and swollen eyes. "Sam..."

"I love you, Jonathan and I probably always will. But I don't think I like the person you've turned out to be." Ducking her head, she squeezed past him toward the master bedroom. "I'm going to get some clothes and go home."

He followed her at a distance. "No, you stay here, I'll leave. I never wanted to hurt you, Samantha. I only wanted to make you happy and give you the life you deserved. I'm sorry if I went about it the wrong way." Without another word, he stumbled down the stairs and out the front door.

Sam watched him go, then went into the master bedroom to change her clothes. Once in the room, she was surrounded by his furniture, his clothes, his scent. He had been staying in the house for almost two weeks, and his presence was everywhere. How could she have misjudged him? How could she have fallen in love with a man who would manipulate her for his own selfish needs?

Jonathan gave little thought to where he was driving. The only place he could really go was to his mother's house. He knew she was home, and knew that he was going to get a lecture, but she was the only support system he had.

Unlocking the front door, he stepped into the foyer and was descended upon almost immediately.

"Jonathan?! What in heaven's name are you doing here?" Alaria asked curiously. She took one look at his face and grabbed for his arm. She led him into the den and pushed him onto the couch. Crossing the room, she poured him a drink, then handed it to him. "What happened?"

He threw back the drink, then groaned loudly. "She found the papers."

Leaning against the desk, she frowned. "Papers?"

"The ones you and I signed for Simon, testifying that the marriage was legitimate." he clarified.

"Oh no." She went to his side and settled onto the cushion next to him. "Did she kick you out?"

"Not really. She wanted to leave... she was so hurt, Mom. The look in her eyes..." he groaned again and dropped his head into his hands. "I couldn't fix it. She'll never forgive me."

"Did you tell her that you love her? Did you explain the whole situation to her? Tell her about all the people who are depending on you for their livelihood?" Alaria asked.

"I told her that I loved her. I told her that the will just pushed me to go out and look for what I wanted. And that she was what I wanted. I offered to sell the company. It didn't matter." he told his mother. "She's really hurting. And I did it."

"Jonathan..." Alaria began, but was interrupted by the phone. Standing, she crossed to the desk and answered the phone. "Hello?" Glancing over at her son, she turned her back to him and spoke quietly. After some soft conversation, she hung up and returned to his side. "That was your wife."

His eyes shot up to meet hers, the word 'wife' hanging in the air. "Is she all right?"

"She called to see if I knew where you were and if you were okay." Alaria answered.

He caught his breath, then released it slowly. "Oh."

"I invited myself over for brunch tomorrow to talk with her and she agreed." she paused. "She obviously still cares about you, darling. Maybe I can help you both."

"She knows that you signed those papers, Mom. She may not be very receptive to you." he warned her.

"Only time will tell, dear. And I can't let this go. I feel responsible for not telling your father what an idiot he was for writing that will." She stroked his hair and smiled sadly. "I thought the world of him, Jonathan, but if he had only known the damage this would cause..."

"You aren't responsible for this, Mom. I should have told her about the will, I should have been honest."

"Go up to sleep, darling. Lets see what the world looks like by the light of the new morning."

Sam opened the front door to let Alaria in.

"Good morning, darling." Alaria pulled the younger woman into a hug, feeling just a hint of resistance.

"Hello."

"I'm so glad you allowed me to come and speak with you. I know you're angry with both Jonathan and me, but I wanted to talk with you."

Nodding, Samantha led her new mother-in-law to the kitchen where the table was set and waiting for them. "There wasn't much in the refrigerator, so I had to make do with fruit, yoghurt, cottage cheese, toast and jellies."

"That's sounds wonderful." Alaria took a seat in the bright breakfast nook.

Sam slid onto a chair, then stared at the food in front of her. She still wasn't hungry. "How... is he all right?"

Alaria clasped her hands together. "How do I answer that, Samantha? He's upset with himself, with his father and me, and he's devastated at having hurt you."

"I suppose you're going to tell me it wasn't his fault."

Pausing to gather her thoughts, Alaria reached for a piece of toast. "I can't say that. I can say it wasn't *only* his fault. There were so many factors at work here, darling, that this was bound to be a mess. I wish it weren't such a big one, though."

"Seeing those papers, and what they really meant, reminded me that I'm the good-for-nothing my step-father told me I was. That no man would ever love me for me. It just reinforced that men only say

187

they love you for their own purposes. And that they rarely ever mean it." Sam said sullenly.

Alaria blinked at the beautiful young woman across from her. "Samantha, believe whatever else you will, but know my son loves you for who you are. He went along with the will only because it fell into his plans with you, not because you fell into the plans for it."

"I don't think I can believe that." she whispered.

"Let me tell you what was really in that will, and what it really meant for Jonathan, and for you." Alaria told her where the will came from and then began to outline its terms. "To gain ownership of the company, Jonathan must begin a family within a year of his marriage. When we had the engagement party, and I found out that you were going back to school, I confronted Jonathan. I asked how he could encourage you to go to school, knowing that you wouldn't be able to have children right away *and* go to school. He basically told me that he was doing what he could to take care of the people in his employ, without jeopardizing the hopes and dreams of the woman he loved. He knew that he would have to deal with a board of directors telling him how to run *his* company, but he could still have a say in how the company moved forward. It meant," she paused. "That good, loyal people would not lose their jobs, their livelihoods. Every decision he made over the past year, was based on balancing his love for you and his responsibility to a company and to *families* that his father founded and cultivated."

"Why didn't he tell me these things months ago?"

Alaria patted her hand. "When would have been a good time to tell you, dear? The first date? The day he proposed? No matter when this came up, it would have caused pain. I think he figured if he kept all the responsibility to himself, no one would be the wiser, or the worse." Smiling gently, she looked Samantha in the eye. "He only wanted to take care of everyone and everything. He's like his father in that way. You have to teach him that you can help him, that you're strong enough. It's not something I did with Frank, though now I wish I had. It would have added an aspect to our relationship that we never had... equality. Frank never blatantly treated me like his inferior, but I was because he had all the knowledge. You need to share everything with each other, no matter how difficult it is. You need to teach Jonathan that, because he never learned that in my house."

"How can we move forward from all of this? My heart still hurts every time I think of the whole episode." Samantha asked.

"You know, Samantha, shortly before Jonathan met you, he came to me and said he wanted the kind of relationship that Frank and I had -- but that he wasn't sure he was capable of that kind of 'great love'. Darling, one person is *not* capable of that kind of great love, it takes two of you. Don't let it get away, no matter what happens. I'll never be able to find someone like Frank again... perhaps someday I may find a companion, but never someone to replace what Frank and I had. Just think of what it would be like to be without him, and I believe you'll realize that you *must* get past the initial hurt... to claim the great love of your life."

It was late afternoon on Monday when the phone rang, startling Samantha from her reverie in the breakfast nook.

"Hello?"

"Um, Mrs. Edwards?"

Sam blinked. "Yes?"

"Hello, this is Miss Patrick." the timid voice trilled.

"I'm sorry, Miss Patrick, but Jonathan isn't here." Why would the shrewd secretary be looking for Jonathan when she knew he was scheduled to be on his honeymoon?

"No, I know he's not." she paused. "He's here."

"Excuse me?"

"I was just going in to water his plants, as I always do on Mondays, and there he was, sitting at his desk like nothing had changed." Miss Patrick's voice lowered to a whisper. "I don't mean to butt in, but he doesn't look very good. And it was my understanding your honeymoon started this morning. Was I wrong?"

"There was a change of plans." Sam said flatly.

"Mrs. Edwards? I've been your husband's secretary for some time now. He was always a wonderful and compassionate boss, but since you've come into his life, he's become a wonderful and caring person. If there's anything I can do to help, please don't hesitate to ask, okay?"

Pausing, Sam listened to the sincerity in the young woman's voice. "Did he say how long he was going to stay?"

"No, he didn't say much at all. He just sat there at his desk, head down, and wouldn't meet my gaze. You know, after he met you, he started smiling all the time and he seemed to realize there was more to our lives, and his, than just business! But now, he just looks so miserable." She cleared her throat, and her voice raised a notch. "I believe he has an appointment available around 4:30 this afternoon, if that is all right with you?"

"All right. I'll come in and speak with him. But don't tell him I'm coming in, okay?" Sam instructed.

"Great, we'll see you then."

The phone went dead in Sam's hand. It was all up to her now, to mend the hurt in her own heart, and move on with her life. Move on with the life she spent so many years dreaming about and praying for as a child. Claim the man who wanted to do nothing more than give it to her.

Sam stepped from the elevator into the reception area of Jon's company. The young woman behind the main desk looked up and smiled. "Good afternoon, Mrs. Edwards. Miss Patrick is expecting you."

Sam smiled wanly and turned down the hall toward Jon's office. As she passed people, they stopped to smile or nod, some greeting her with a cheerful, "Good afternoon, Mrs. Edwards." As she approached Miss Patrick's desk, Sam really began to understand the closeness of the people in this particular company. When she had first approached Jon's office, she had been so aware of herself and her discomfort, that she never noticed how friendly and warm the people around her were. No one was staring at her in disgust or dismay, they were greeting her with open arms, as a new and welcome part of their family. What else could Jon have done besides fight for their survival, in whatever way he knew how?

"Mrs. Edwards." Miss Patrick stood and came around from behind her desk to hug Sam. "I'm so glad you're here. He hasn't left his office all day and refused lunch!" she whispered furiously. "I was so worried about him!"

Sam hugged the woman back. "I'm going to try and take care of him, Miss Patrick, I promise." Straightening her shoulders, she asked, "Is he expecting an appointment?"

"Yes, he's actually expecting Ron from accounting." Miss Patrick grinned. "I bet you're a welcome sight in his place."

"Let's hope so." She paused and looked back at the pretty secretary. "Thank you for your help. I appreciate it more than I can say. Why don't you go home early... I think we may be here for a while."

"Are you sure you don't need me to stay?"

Sam shook her head. "I think it's all up to us, now."

"Good luck." Miss Patrick gave her the thumbs up, then grabbed her purse from a drawer and scurried away.

Without knocking, Sam opened the heavy door and stepped into the bright office. Just as quietly, she shut the door behind her, noting that Jon's chair was turned to face out the window. There was no going back, no chickening out now. "Jon?"

The chair swivelled around slowly and he stared at her uncomprehendingly. "Samantha?"

She nodded, but didn't move.

"Is that really you? Because I've seen you in my daydreams before."

"It's me. I'm really here. And I swear to you, I'm not leaving this office alone." she promised him.

"I don't understand."

"I think that's the big problem, here. I didn't understand what you really had to do, and you didn't understand that I need to be involved in *our* life decisions." She stepped forward, but didn't take a seat. "Jon, I'm a strong and independent woman and I need to be involved in what happens in *our* life. I'm not going to be like your mother... I don't want to sit back and go along for the ride."

"I don't want you to be like my mother. I want you for the person that you are, independence and all."

"Then you have to trust me with everything. No matter how difficult it is." she pleaded, her arms outstretched toward him. "You need to share your life with me and let me be an equal partner in this relationship."

"I want to do that, Samantha. But I didn't know how to tell you..."

"I understand that now, Jon." she interrupted. "I'm not saying our life is going to be easy, but it *has* to be equal between us."

He got up from his chair and came around the front of his desk, stopping just a step away from her. "What does this mean for us, Samantha? Because I don't think I could live without you."

"I want to move forward with our life together, Jon. I know there's some hurt between us, but I hope it will make our love stronger. I don't want to lose the great love of my life because of a misunderstanding." she told him.

One more step and he was closing his arms around her. "I love you so much, Samantha. Having to walk out of that house was the hardest thing I've ever had to do in my life."

"Letting you go was the hardest for me. I'm thankful that your mother was so up-front and honest with me. And I'm thankful that your secretary was so caring and sneaky." she grinned as he pulled away from her.

"You mean she set me up?" he asked incredulously, his dark eyebrows drawing downward.

"Miss Patrick really was very helpful. She called me and convinced me to come in to see you."

"Then I must send her some flowers on our way to the airport tonight." he nodded vigorously.

"Airport?"

He caught her up in his arms again, grinning from ear to ear. "Sweetie, we have a honeymoon to catch!"